Draw me a Hero

N K ASHWORTH

Draw me a Hero

Lemon Ink,
an imprint of Lasavia Publishing Ltd.
Auckland, New Zealand

www.lasaviapublishing.com

Cover art and interior illustrations by Roger Mason
looksgoodonpaper.co.uk

Cover design by Kate Ashworth

ISBN: 978-0-9951398-5-5

for Kim

Acknowledgements

It takes an author to write a story, but a whole team to create a book. So this is a big appreciative shout-out to all the crew at Lasavia Publishing without whom this book would never have existed. And my grateful thanks to Roger Mason, 'artist extraordinaire', who provided me with the wonderful internal illustrations and the stunning cover image. A special thank you to my daughter Kate, who read it first, went real easy on any criticism, and inspired me to clad my novel's heroine in a flying helmet. Finally, an acknowledgement that this tale is not only about superheroes; it also deals with the relationship between sisters. This one is for you, Sis.

Contents

Superhero

There is a superhero standing in our kitchen doorway. I've spent the morning drawing him, and now he's come to life... complete with long grey trenchcoat, blue jeans, red converse and a white tee. Seriously cute.

He strolls casually across the peeling black and white tiled floor to where I'm sitting at our old rimu table. Breakfast remains were hastily shoved aside an hour ago to make way for my meagre art supplies: half an HB pencil with a chewed top, a large sketchbook with battered corners and an incomplete set of pastels that I'd picked up in an art shop bargain bin. There are no greens, so I'm carefully avoiding any depictions of grass.

The superhero looks down at my drawing and says, "You're very good at art." His voice is deep and slightly raspy. My knees are not the only part of my anatomy currently out of sync.

"Er... thanks. What did you say your name was?"

He gives me a slow mocking smile and tosses a lock of his untidy black hair from his piercing brown eyes. Just like the character in my drawing.

Finally, he replies, "I didn't. But you may call me Proton."

That figures. It's the name of my superhero — the one in my picture. Actually, it's plastered all over my sketch in huge black letters: **PROTON**. The same sketch that's sitting in full view on the table.

Suddenly Proton grins. "Sorry! Couldn't resist teasing you... My real name is Bailey Summer — just moved in with my family three doors down. Any chance I can scrounge some milk off you guys?"

Oh God. Now I feel like a total idiot — and I'm talking World Class Idiot here. To hide my confusion and the growing flush on my face, I go to the fridge. It's almost empty — no surprises there. Mum is out doing the weekly supermarket shop. Luckily for him, there is a new two-litre container of blue-top milk in the door compartment. I carefully pour half into a liberally chipped china jug and hand him the plastic container. His long tapered fingers briefly touch mine. I swear I feel a burst of electricity.

He gives me another lazy smile. "So what did you say your name was?"

I look at him innocently. "I didn't. But you may call me Taker."

"Taker? That's unusual. What's your surname?"

"Hike."

"Taker Hike," he repeats and then bursts out laughing. I can still hear his laughter as he walks out the door and off down the street.

"Jane, who was that you were talking to?" asks Mum, appearing in the doorway, her arms laden with groceries from Pak 'n Save.

"Some new kid called Bailey Summer. His family have moved in three doors down. Wanted to borrow milk. A total jerk."

"I hope they don't make a habit of it. I'm not working two jobs just to feed half the neighbourhood."

She dumps the supermarket bags down onto the table.

Mum is a solo parent. She's a cleaner at Malvern High School (*my* high school... embarrassing doesn't even begin to describe it) and does weekend shifts at the local rest home. She looks permanently stressed and this year a definite line has started to appear between her eyes. She glares down at my sketch.

"Is this school work?"

She knows it isn't.

"Nah. It's a design for a competition at Auckland Libraries to create a superhero."

The line gets deeper.

"Well, it sounds like a total waste of time to me. You should be focusing on all your other school work. Take a leaf out of your sister's book for a change."

Yeah, right... as if I'm ever going to be able to compete

with Saint Madeleine. That's my sister — Madeleine Annabel Dawson. I call her Mad for short. It's not only short for Madeleine; it's all her initials put together (Mum was having a 'blonde' moment). Mad's two years older than me and one of those people who at sixteen has everything: tall, blonde like Mum, athletic and academically a straight-A student. Get the picture?

As for me, I'm short with mouse-coloured hair, wear glasses, and I'm hopelessly average. The only thing I excel at is art, and that has no value in Mum's eyes. I don't even have a middle name. Just plain Jane Dawson. Apparently, Mum couldn't think of one and had to hurry up and complete the forms so she could apply for the Domestic Purposes Benefit.

Plain Jane — says it all really.

I've never met my father. He buggered off when I was still in Mum's womb and Mad was barely a toddler. Mad says she remembers him, but I think it's just wishful thinking. *Hello! Who remembers stuff from when they were two?*

I've seen her pouring over a photo of him holding her on his lap. She looks predictably cute in the photo; all chubby cheeks and blonde ringlets. *Ladies and gentleman, may I present the winner of Pakuranga's Most Gorgeous Toddler Competition!*

He looks, well... average... nondescript. The sort of guy that gets overlooked in a police line-up: shoulder-length light brown hair and wearing a smile that doesn't quite touch his eyes, like he wishes he was miles away. Last we heard he was in Aussie. Guess he got his wish.

I look down at my drawing and give an exaggerated sigh. I

trace my right forefinger down my character's long nose and let it rest lightly on his parted lips, careful not to smudge the pencil lines. *Right about now I could do with a superhero in my life*, I think miserably. The sketch looks back up at me, giving an all too familiar mocking smile.

"Jane Dawson, you're late!" shouts my form teacher the next morning.

I'm aware the whole class is staring — waiting to hear today's excuse. Punctuality is not exactly my strong point, but my justifications are usually highly creative and, according to Facebook comments posted by classmates (*so dope, rad, sick Jane!*), they do at least have entertainment value.

"Sorry, Mr Shields, Mum's car broke down. Then Mum and my sister went all Chernobyl on me, because flames started flying out of the bonnet. We were miles from the nearest bus stop, but a police car appeared, flashing like a—"

"I'm not interested in your personal dramas. *Not interested!* Everyone else has managed to get to school on time. I've moved you to the front of the class; we have a new student joining us today. And if you are late once more this week, Jane, you will stay behind on Friday for detention. *Detention!*"

Bugger. I hate detentions. The ultimate in How to Waste Everybody's Time and Cause Maximum Resentment and Achieve Absolutely Nothing.

I look across at Mr Shields. He's hardly intimidating. He's old and wrinkly, and has an irritating tendency to repeat key words. But he doesn't make idle threats.

I zip the rest of my excuse and sit down meekly in front of the one available desk. For the record, there really were flames coming out of the car bonnet. And Mum and Mad did lose the plot, but I quickly put the fire out using water from my drink bottle. The arrival of the policeman was pure wishful thinking on my part. There are no superheroes zooming to the rescue in our lives.

I look back at my usual seat only to find none other than Bailey Summer giving me a lopsided grin. *Well, isn't that just hunky-dory...* I glare at him, which only has the effect of widening his grin.

At lunchtime, I head outside and find a quiet bench to sit at. Don't get me wrong: I'm not a total social disaster. I just don't feel like having my face rubbed in other teens' flashy smartphones. Mine's a basic Warehouse El Cheapo model. Not the sort you want to brandish in a public place. Especially one frequented by judgemental peers.

Bailey strolls over to my bench. No trenchcoat but he still manages to look cool and nonchalant in Malvern High's stuffy grey uniform. *How is that even possible?*

"Listen, J.D. Think we may have got off to a bad start..."

"My name is Jane."

"J.D. sounds cooler, don't you think?"

"Drop dead!"

"Now that's what I like about you, J.D. You're very direct. No mixed signals."

I deliberately ignore him and carry on eating my lunch: ham, Colby cheese and lettuce with the bread buttered right to the very edges. I know, because Mum always makes them like that. Same boring lunch every day. And Oreos, of course. Alternating between chocolate and vanilla filling, depending on what I ate yesterday. Today is a vanilla day. So predictable. My life's predictable... *boring, boring, boring.*

Bailey casually reaches a hand across and removes one of my sandwiches from its plastic container. I yell, "What the—"

Too late — it's already in his mouth.

"Sorry, J.D. Automatic reflex around food. So where were we?"

I narrow my eyes to thin slits. "You were about to drop dead."

"God — I like that! Proton, the long lost son of the Lord Protector who can destroy his enemies with just one look..." He pulls a notepad out of his pocket and furiously starts writing.

"What the hell are you doing?" I demand.

"Writing. Did I forget to mention I'm a writer? Oh, and by the way, love your name 'Proton' for a superhero. I can work with that. It's the Greek word for 'first'. Did you know that?"

"No," I reply, through gritted teeth.

It goes straight over his head.

"So, J.D. Now all we need to decide is the name of our superhero's arch-enemy. Any suggestions?"

I ignore his use of the word *our* and say sarcastically, "I have a sister, Madeleine, who would fit the roll perfectly."

"Mmm... sibling rivalry, Cain and Abel — the mark of Cain... Perfect!"

"What?" I can't keep up with this guy. *Is he for real?*

"Here, let me run it all past you. Proton, the long lost son of the Lord Protector, is the only survivor of his planet after it was destroyed by the people of Kane — spelt K.A.N.E. He escapes to planet Earth and his only weapon of protection is the power of his gaze. He must stay hypervigilant, constantly aware there are people out there who carry the mark of Kane and will stop at nothing to hunt him down. So what do you think, J.D.?"

"I think you are certifiable and if your wandering hand strays any closer to my remaining ham, cheese and lettuce sandwich, I shall personally cut it off."

"I knew you'd like it! So that should give you enough info to make a start."

I know I'm going to regret asking, but I can't resist. "Start what?"

"Our graphic novel, of course. The one that will be a huge success worldwide and launch both our careers; yours as an artist and mine as a writer."

And on that note Bailey Summer gets up and saunters off, leaving me alone on the school bench with my mouth gaping so wide you could run a tank through it.

Aviator Hat

"Who was that guy at school I saw you hanging around today?"

I should feel flattered Mad even noticed. Usually she's got her head stuck in a book, or she's pounding the pavements in her running shoes, head down, grimly determined. But I don't feel in the least bit flattered. I feel defensive.

"*He* was hanging around *me*," I snap. "I wasn't hanging around him. What's it to you anyway?"

Mad shrugs her slender shoulders. "He looked... very mature. Not your usual type. Just take care okay?"

Whoa! Back up here. So what exactly does she mean by

my usual type? I'm hardly dating material. No guy at school has even shown the slightest interest in me. But all I say is, "Whatever."

Actually, now I *am* a little flattered. Mad's playing the protective Big Sister role and thinks there could be something going on between mousey me and Bailey Summer, newly appointed Class Hunk. Nice!

Eager to maintain the illusion, I decide to humour Bailey and spend the evening sketching a trench-coated superhero in various poses. He needed hero-ing up a bit so he now sports a snazzy iconic *P* on his white t-shirt. Every time Mum walks past, I quickly cover the images with my maths book. It does nothing to improve my maths, but by the end of the evening, I have a wad of drawings and super-fast reflexes.

The next day Bailey strolls over at lunchtime. I casually produce my drawings.

"Mmm..." he says, his dark eyebrows drawn together in a frown.

I feel irrationally deflated and reply, "They're no good then?"

"Hell, J.D. They're not just good, they're brilliant! It's just... I had imagined Proton with some sort of disfigurement."

I produce a pencil and my hand hovers over the sketches. "Are we talking 'Harry Potter' type scar here or some major physical deformity?"

"Mmm... how about third-degree burns to his upper arms and torso?"

I give a dramatic sigh, slowly put down my pencil and say, "For God's sake! The guy is wearing a trenchcoat — he won't *look* any different."

"Ah, now that's where you're wrong, J.D. The burns were caused by Proton's unsuccessful attempt to rescue his family during the Kanine War — the Great War that also destroyed his planet. The anguish and horror will show deep in his eyes."

Something makes me look up at Bailey, only to find his brown eyes effectively hidden behind a dark pair of sunnies. I wonder if the corners of his eyes are crinkled in amusement or clouded by grief. I shake my head. This guy is really starting to get to me.

I look back down at the sketches, aware he is standing so close I can even smell his aftershave. He must shave... Mad is right, he *is* mature. The smell reminds me of the ocean, salt spray and wild, windswept secluded beaches... I am having trouble focusing.

I give an exasperated, "Tsk," and quietly alter Proton's eyes, enlarging the pupils and subtly shifting the set of the eyebrows.

Bailey watches. When I have finished, he looks down and says in a cracked whisper, "Perfect."

I feel a wave of pleasure sweep over me.

Then he looks across at my lunchbox and breaks the moment altogether by commenting, "Is it just my imagination, or are there enough sandwiches for two today?"

I hand over half the sandwiches. "If you must know, my sister Madeleine dumped hers in my box this morning — apparently she's on some kind of special diet. Don't get used to the idea: her diets never last."

"Madeleine's that tall blonde in year twelve?"

I look up at him again. His expression is impossible to read; damn those sunnies. And now he knows who my sister is — *Saint Madeleine wins life's lottery once again.* I don't even bother making an effort to keep the sourness out of my tone and say, "Yeah... I know. Hard to imagine we are sisters, isn't it?"

Bailey gives me an enigmatic smile and then focuses on demolishing his sandwiches.

As the bell goes for the start of afternoon classes, he suddenly hands over several sheets of paper from his notebook, saying, "You'll need these."

"And what are *these* exactly?"

"It's called a storyboard," he explains patiently. "That's how graphic novels start off. Pages with the dialogue between characters and basic thumbnail sketches to show the artist what images are needed."

I glance down at his crude stick figures arranged in various sized boxes. In my head I keep seeing an image of Bailey and Mad together. They are holding hands and Mad is looking up into his eyes with an adoring look. I hate the image. I snap, "Drawing isn't exactly your strong point, is it?"

He gives me an amused smile and says, "That's why we make such a good team, J.D." Then he strolls off, leaving me once again with my mouth wide open.

Only one word in my head has registered. I am thinking, *Bailey and I are a team. A TEAM! No more Plain Jane. It's cool J.D... part of a team with Bailey Summer.* I feel like I'm gliding to the rest of my classes on a hover-board.

This evening, I curl up on my bed and pull my old leather aviator hat firmly around my ears. I picked the hat up at a local charity shop a year ago and Mum calls it my 'Thing'. *'Why have you got that Thing on your head again, Jane?'* She really doesn't get it. Personally, I think it looks seriously cool in a Steampunk sort of way, and it even has sewn-on earpieces and a separate chin strap. And I love the smell. A combination of leather and neatsfoot oil which I rub in to stop the leather going dry. Best of all, the aviator hat helps me focus. Sounds bizarre, but it's almost as if it can block out the world around me and channel my energy inwards.

I reach across for my school bag and grab Bailey's storyboard. I idly start to read his words. He writes in capitals and they are messy. And I mean *really* messy. His *m*'s, *n*'s and *w*'s all look remarkably similar and everything is slightly angled to the right as if his words struggle to catch up with his thoughts.

As I decipher the dialogue between his characters, I feel a rude jolt of surprise. Almost like Bailey had just walked in and kicked me in the stomach. I sit up straighter and turn another page. The brutal kicks keep coming. I swallow. This isn't what I'd been expecting. I feel like a skydiver who has been pushed out of an aircraft before he is ready to jump — my thoughts and feelings flay around in panic. The world Bailey describes is raw and brutal — a million light-years away from the safe cocoon of my own boring and predictable existence.

His words create in my mind's eye the world of Proton. It's almost as if I can see the things Proton has seen, feel the things he has felt and hear the sounds he has heard. The shocking loss of his whole family in a fireball of flames at the end of the first chapter really affects me. I hug my knees tightly and by the time I have read about the total destruction of Proton's planet, I have to reach over to clutch Big Ted, my old childhood teddy. I haven't felt the need to do that in yonks.

In fact, I think the last time I cuddled Big Ted, our old black and white cat, Domino, had just died. I must have been pretty small because I can remember asking Mum, two days later, if we could dig him up and take him to the vets — I even offered to pay for his 'treatment' with my pocket money. I remember Mum sat me down, put a caring arm around my shoulders and gently gave me a reality check. By the time she had finished talking, I had grasped the awful finality of death.

Reading Bailey's words gives me that same sense of desperate finality. I am caught up in a realm of intense emotion but how much of it is Proton's and how much is Bailey Summer's, I have absolutely no idea.

I pick up my sketchbook, sharpen a pencil and start to map out some basic illustrations. I lose all sense of time and it's after midnight when I finally remember that tomorrow is a school day — I need to get some 'beauty' sleep; *funny ha-ha*. But even when I take off the old aviator hat and lay my head down on my pillow, I am still flying through the air on a rocket ship feeling desperately scared and alone.

Inferno

The following Sunday Bailey knocks on our front door. I know it's him because of the distinctive tall trench-coated shadow through the glass. I feel ridiculously nervous. I hang back and let Mum answer and then eavesdrop from the safety of the hallway; I position myself so I can see and hear him but he can't see or hear me.

I'm wearing my Thing again. At times like this it's perfect to hide under and I feel safer: irrational, I know... but I'm a teenager — what do you expect? I'm also feeling kind of smug that Mad decided to go for a run ten minutes earlier. If she does suddenly appear, I figure she will be reeking of sweat and her ample breasts will be hidden under her baggy sweatshirt. Last week Gordon Ainsley, in year 9, yelled out that my sister scored the watermelons and I had the pips. *Moron.*

"Good morning, Mrs Dawson!" says Bailey, reaching his hand out to shake hers firmly. "I've recently moved into the neighbourhood and wondered if you had any chores you need a hand with. I can mow your lawn for you, chop wood, wash the car..."

"You must be Bailey; Jane mentioned your family had moved into the Petersons' place. I hadn't realised they'd sold it. I thought they were on a three-month cruise around Europe?"

"My mum's a distant relative," he replies smoothly. "Our house was one of the ones red-stickered after the Christchurch earthquake. There's been endless problems with the insurance pay-out and rebuild, so the Petersons said we could stay at their place. It's just temporary."

At the mention of Christchurch, Mum's whole face softens but she still turns down his offer. "Unfortunately, Bailey, I don't earn enough to pay anyone to help out around the place."

Another missed opportunity. *The story of my life...*

Bailey looks out at the tangled mass of daisies happily growing on our lawn and then flashes her a charming smile. "Tell you what, Mrs Dawson, I'll run over with the mower once a week, and do some weeding, if you supply the petrol and shout me Sunday lunch."

I hold my breath.

Mum laughs, "Don't your parents feed you?"

I'm seriously starting to wonder the same thing, but Bailey just shrugs and replies, "My folks are in the theatre and work odd hours. Sundays I'm left to my own devices — it tends to be baked beans on toast."

Mum smiles, "Well, I'm sure I can do better than that. We usually have a lunch-time roast on Sundays, so how about we make it a deal. When would you like to start?"

He grins, "How does today sound?"

She walked right into that one. I grin too.

Mum throws back her head, laughing. I suddenly realise this is the first time I've seen her laugh in ages. "It's a deal," she says. "I'll get Jane to peel some extra potatoes."

I stop grinning.

So that's how Bailey ended up coming around on a regular basis. Every Sunday, come rain or shine, he starts up our old mower around eleven o'clock and methodically walks back and forth, leaving careful lines across our garden. Othertimes he weeds around the rose bushes or cleans out the goldfish pond until finally Mad or I call him in for lunch.

Surprisingly, Mad seems wary of Bailey. She cuts short his attempts at conversation and I start to think she is playing hard to get; the lure of unavailability and all that. Then this morning I swear she deliberately walks in on us while he's discussing new scenes in our graphic novel. Two's company, three's a crowd; I make a point of glaring at her furiously. Times like this I really wish I was an only child.

During lunch I see him reach across and say something

quietly to her at the table. She jerks her head up in surprise. Afterwards, she seems different around him, relaxed, laughing at his jokes — her eyes warmer. I wonder what he'd said. When I ask her, she goes all coy and mutters, "It's private."

I decide to be direct and ask Bailey at school the next day.

"Madeleine was worried about all the time I'm spending with you." He gives me a devilish grin and adds, "For some reason she didn't trust me."

"So how *exactly* did you put my sister's mind at rest?"

He tilts his head slightly and looks across at me, almost like he is sizing me up. A shadow falls across his face. But his only comment is: "That's for me to know and you to wonder..."

God, he can be infuriating.

This Sunday is Labour weekend and the midday sun is scorching; the sort of heat you would normally expect after Christmas, not in October. Summer is invading spring, with a bit of help from climate change. I look out the window while I'm peeling the vegetables at the sink, careful not to splash my carefully ironed blouse (ironed, I confess, for Bailey's benefit).

Perfect timing; Bailey is stripping off his white t-shirt. I can only see his back view and experience a rather guilty and delicious pleasure as my eyes follow the rippling of his muscles as he pushes our old mower down the lawn. *The sun isn't the only thing that's hot out there today. And I mean seriously HOT!*

A sheen of sweat emphasizes his bulging biceps. Perhaps he works out. Maybe I could join the same gym? We could do push-ups together. *Mmm...*

Then he turns around at the bottom of the garden to come back up, and I suck in my breath. The large potato I am peeling *plops* into the sink splashing muddy water all the way up my blouse. I no longer care.

I keep repeating, "Shit! Shit! *SHIT!*"

It's so unexpected. My perfect teenage fantasy has been brutally interrupted. It's as if a sculptor had only half-finished carving Bailey's body from marble, paying exquisite attention to creating a perfectly smooth, beautiful face and back, like some Greek God-like Adonis, but then left his upper frontal body with crudely-hacked, deep and ugly chisel marks.

There are a series of so-called slave or prisoner sculptures by Michelangelo, dating back to the sixteenth century — that's who Bailey reminds me of. The front of his chest and upper arms are horribly disfigured. The skin is puckered like old leather and in places it's a raw and livid red, like butcher's meat.

I guess they are burns and I give an involuntary shudder. It's hard not to imagine the extreme pain as the burns started to heal. Though I once read that severe third-degree burns are actually less painful than second-degree, because of the damage to all the nerve endings. Perhaps Bailey had been placed in a medically induced coma to save him from the worst of the trauma. I hope to God that was the case. I also wonder if he is still having skin-graft operations — some of those wounds look redder than others.

I don't say anything to Bailey when he finally comes inside for lunch. What could I say? I confess, his disfigurement makes him feel more... *reachable* for a Plain Jane like myself. Does that make sense? Plus, I've always had a weakness for the walking wounded. I guess that's why I insisted we adopt Tripod, the three-legged ginger cat at the SPCA that nobody else wanted (after finally accepting that Domino, our old black and white moggy, was never going to be like Lazarus).

I think of Proton. How he lost his whole family in a fiery inferno. They couldn't be resurrected either. It begins to dawn on me: Is Bailey's graphic novel actual fantasy or is it based on appalling reality?

Ladyhawke

It's after lunch on Sunday and we are going over Bailey's latest storyboard.

He suddenly announces, "Did you know you have the most amazing blue eyes?"

I can feel myself turning bright red and try to laugh off his unexpected comment.

"Yeah, right. All four of them."

"There's nothing wrong with glasses, J.D. But have you considered contacts?" and he carries on talking about the storyboard as if nothing has happened.

I don't think it's a coincidence my annual optician's appointment is coming up on Friday. In our kitchen we have one of those fridges that is colourfully plastered in garish fridge magnets and reminder notes. My appointment was in full view while Bailey had tucked into his Sunday roast.

So come Friday it's almost inevitable I tentatively ask for contacts. I do it in front of the optician so Mum can't make too big a deal about the extra cost. She doesn't like people knowing we struggle financially.

A week later I am finally able to pick them up and nervously try them out for the first time. Mum does a double-take. "Goodness, Jane. I'd forgotten how absolutely stunning your eyes are! Those contacts are worth every cent." My face flushes with pleasure.

Back at school for the afternoon lessons, I confess I'm looking forward to Bailey's reaction. The bell has just rung to signify the end of lunch and it's the usual madhouse; kids scattering like Jaffas in a cinema. But there is Bailey, still glued to our regular bench-seat. I stroll over, trying hard to look casual.

I can tell by his intense expression that he is lost in Proton's world. His dark eyebrows are drawn together with that familiar look of pain haunting his eyes. I give an awkward cough. He ignores me. I cough again — louder this time. Finally, he looks up, stares a fraction longer than usual, blinks and then finishes off the sentence he is writing.

Talk about a let-down.

The next morning I am home alone. Mum works a day shift at the Twilight Years Rest Home in Pakuranga on Saturdays (I call it the *Twilight Zone*) and Mad is out pounding the pavements as usual. I'm sitting on our old couch, with its springs poking up in inconvenient places, feeling bored, neglected and more than a little sorry for myself.

The front doorbell rings. I almost don't answer it, in case it's Jehovah's Witnesses. Then I see the familiar tall shadow and realise it's just Bailey.

I open the door and say sourly, "We haven't stocked up the fridge yet from your last visit."

"And a good morning to you too, J.D.! I've come bearing gifts."

I look suspiciously at his small plastic bag as he comes inside. There appear to be two objects; one is obviously a DVD and the other is... God knows. Bailey quickly shoves the mystery object into his coat pocket, carefully removes the shiny disc from the DVD case and inserts it into our player.

"Any popcorn?" he asks hopefully.

I confess I'm intrigued. I decide to humour him and put a large bowl of popcorn in the microwave. When it's ready I place it between us on the couch and then curl up against the worn cushions. The thing with Bailey is that I never know exactly what he is going to come out with next. He's infuriating at times but never boring. He adds a totally new dimension to the word *unpredictable*. There is no doubt in my mind that Saturday morning has taken an abrupt turn for the better. I tell him to hit 'Play'.

To be honest, I'm not really sure what to expect. I confess I'm hoping he's got an Adults Only movie out from some sleazy video shop (do they even exist now?) to put me in the mood for an elaborate seduction.

He hasn't.

True, it *is* a movie about love, but not the cheap 'wam, bam, thank you, Mam' type Mad had once warned me about. This is a movie about True Love — the sort that lasts forever and continues even when the woman is a hawk by day and her lover is a wolf by night. So, effectively, they are doomed never to be together as man and woman.

It is, of course, that classic eighties movie *Ladyhawke* and I love it to bits. And I love sharing it with Bailey, watching his hand straying freely into the popcorn only centimetres from mine and feeling flattered that he wants to share this special love story with me. *This*, I think naively, *is the best day of my fourteen-year-old life...*

As the movie finishes and the credits start to roll, Bailey looks across at me and says, "Well?"

I look back at him, through contacts that have misted over slightly with the intense emotion of the ending, and I start to enthuse: about the stunning scenery, the humour in some of the dialogue (Matthew Broderick is sooo cute), and even the haunting Gregorian chants. Right now I feel like I'm floating in heaven, especially as Bailey's arm is currently around me *(okay, so it's actually resting on the back of the couch – but that's a mere technicality)*.

"You've totally missed the point, J.D."

"What?"

"Here, I'll spell it out for you." Bailey grabs the remote and hits 'scene select'. An image of Michelle Pfeiffer appears on the screen. Her head is out of the mysterious hooded cloak and she is giving a gentle smile to the camera.

I am still puzzled and say, "Sorry, I don't get it."

Bailey gives a long-suffering sigh. "Her hair, J.D. Check out her hair!"

I look again. Her hair is very short and has an elfin quality. Being Michelle Pfeiffer she does naturally look gorgeous. I still can't see where he's going with this, so I say, "What about her hair?"

Bailey rolls his eyes and reaches across to grab my ponytail. It's a long braided ponytail and I can't remember the last time my hair was cut. Hair is not my strong point. I religiously brush it each morning, scrape it back into a tight plait and then forget about it for the next twenty-four hours.

The only time I've paid more than casual attention to my mouse-coloured locks was the time we had 'visitors'. That's what Mum calls them. She hates it if I use the word *nits*.

Before the 'visitors' I used to regularly wear my hair loose, but since then I scrape it back, just in case the dreaded guests decide to swing by again.

I am conscious Bailey has got my plait in his hand. I am just about to pull it away from him when he reaches into his coat pocket, removes a pair of slender sharp scissors, and promptly slices through it.

It appears to happen in slow motion. For a few seconds I

look down in paralyzed horror at the woven strands of brown hair now laying in his hands, totally unattached to their owner — me. When it eventually comes, my scream is piercing, and out of the corner of my eye I even see the neighbour's cat, who I always thought was deaf, take off like a bullet across our lawn.

Then I whisper, with venom dripping from every syllable, *"What—have—you— done?"*

Bailey doesn't even have the decency to look apologetic. He simply shrugs and says, "Trust me, J.D. I know what I'm doing."

I reply through gritted teeth, "Bailey Summer, you have just *ruined* my LIFE!"

"Now calm down, J.D. I have the situation under total control."

As he says the word *control*, I start to lose it. Having spent my anger, I now feel my face crumple and I swallow a sob. I open my mouth again, but my words are dissolved in a tsunami of tears. I am barely conscious of him gently guiding me over to the kitchen sink and placing my head under the warm flow of the mixer tap. At some point I smell apricots and fresh garden herbs (our shampoo and conditioner never match) and I become aware I am sitting on our low kitchen stool with a thin red-checked tea-towel around my shoulders.

More surprising is the quiet confidence of Bailey's fingers as they nimbly dance across my scalp; a *snip* here and a *snip-snap* there. My tears have run dry and now there is only the occasional heartfelt sob. All that is going through my mind is how could the best day of my life turn so dramatically into the worst possible one, and, more importantly: how was I ever

going to face the kids in my class on Monday morning.

Then finally the movement of his fingers stop, and he asks for a hairdryer.

"Third drawer down, on the right," I reply numbly.

Seconds later the dryer is making yet another assault on all of my senses. Eventually there's silence. Bailey removes the tea-towel with a matador's flourish. I find myself propelled over to the large ornate mirror above the mantelpiece; yet another op-shop score. I deliberately scrunch up my eyes in denial.

"Open them," he whispers.

"Bugger off," I whisper back.

He chuckles, "Only after you open your eyes."

Finally, I ease them open.

I gasp.

I am startled by the apparition that stares back at me.

My large almond-shaped blue eyes are perfectly framed by a waiflike bob of brown hair.

Okay, so I may still be a bit flat-chested, but, as far as my face and hair are concerned, I am now capable of giving Michelle Pfeiffer some stiff competition!

"So was I right or was I *right*..."

"Bailey Summer," I say with wonder in my voice, "You *were* right and all is forgiven."

I swear I see his eyes well up before he turns away.

Green-Eyed Monster

When Mum comes home, she is blown away by my haircut. She insists on baking a huge batch of chocolate chip cookies and asks me to take them round to Bailey.

"See if he'd mind cutting my hair tomorrow instead of doing the lawns."

Oh God. Sometimes she can be *so* embarrassing. I decide not to make a fuss though; I've been dying for an excuse to meet Bailey's parents. They've been living at the Petersons' for almost a month now and I've never even caught sight of them. Bailey says his dad is an actor and his mum's a makeup artist —

I guess that's where he learnt to do hair and stuff.

The Petersons' house is a boring two-storey eighties creation with cream concrete blocks below, pale brown fibrolite weatherboards above, all topped by dark brown roof tiles. It closely resembles a chocolate dipped caramel ice-cream, complete with 'flake' chimney. When there is no reply to the doorbell, I peer through the glass door panel that runs vertically alongside. Everywhere looks incredibly tidy and I quickly rub my nose smears off the polished surface.

Undeterred, I venture around to the back of the house. Its quarter-acre section is in immaculate condition; not a blade of grass out of place and the concrete path looks as though it has recently been water blasted. I am about to knock on the ranch-slider but something makes me reach across and once again press my nose up to the glass.

I can just make out Bailey sitting on a leather couch. His head is in his hands and his shoulders are heaving up and down. I can see the irregular flickering light of a television set and I assume he's cracking up with laughter. I want to share the joke. I'm about to yell out some smart-arsed comment when I suddenly realise he's not laughing at all. He's *crying*. I step back abruptly, feeling like a voyeur.

Then I reach forward again and carefully wipe away the smudges on the glass where my nose has been. The biscuits are on a plate and sealed in a plastic bag. I return to the front door and quietly tie the bag to the door handle.

Back at home, I decide to send him a text message.

Should be a simple enough exercise.

It isn't.

The thing is, I want to sound cool and use the latest teen lingo. Which basically means emojis; that twenty-first-century equivalent of Egyptian hieroglyphics. And like their ancient cousins, emojis are enigmatic and incomprehensible — the perfect antidote to hovering parents. Saves us having to write PIR (parents in room). But Bailey is a wordsmith, so I suspect cute symbols will leave him cold. So I decide to opt for a more traditional approach and use textspeak. However, any textspeak that was cool last year now sounds lame. Worse still, parents are actually using them. Besides, there are no texting acronyms that cover what I need to say anyway. Eventually I settle on: *mum <3 my hair ☺ check out front door & will u cut hers 2morrow instead of lawns? rotflol! JD*

He replies almost immediately, *okey doke & thanks for cookies! what's rotflol??*

I've learnt two things about Bailey from his reply. He's probably an Indiana Jones fan, and he knows even less than I do about textspeak. I feel relieved and reply: *rolling on the floor and laughing out loud!*

I bet he's not doing either.

He's probably still crying.

I wish I knew why.

The next day Bailey turns up at the usual time but comes straight through into the kitchen. Mum is all girlish and excited and they start discussing possible styles. I feel like an intruder.

"Ready, Mrs Dawson?" he finally asks, his scissors poised just above her head.

"Ready as I'll ever be!" laughs Mum nervously, adding, "But please call me Laura."

Oh God, this is even more mortifying than I'd imagined — now they are on a first name basis. Neither of them seem to be aware of my presence.

"So tell me, Laura," says Bailey. "When you were my age, what did *you* want to be when you grew up?"

"Honestly?"

"Uh-huh." Bailey is already snipping away now, his long fingers gliding confidently across Mum's scalp.

"I wanted to be a librarian. I was a total bookworm as a teenager and always reading. I couldn't imagine anything more wonderful than being surrounded by books."

"So what happened?"

"At eighteen, I met Madeleine and Jane's father and became pregnant. We married, despite both our parent's vehement opposition. They said we were far too young and needed to continue our education. But we were in love and determined to prove them all wrong."

"And did you?"

Mum turns her head around and gives Bailey a wry look. "I'm divorced and clean other people's toilets for a living. What do you think?"

Bailey chuckles and replies, "I think, Laura, you need to remember your original dream. Dreams don't come with an expiry date like supermarket yoghurts."

At this point I leave the room. I don't think either of them notices. I'm aware I am partly jealous Mum is getting all of Bailey's attention, but what disturbs me even more, is thinking of Mum as a person separate to me with unfulfilled yearnings. She has never talked to me about that stuff. True, there are plenty of books in our house, but I seldom catch her reading any of them. I guess she just doesn't have the time.

Mum originally took on the cleaning job at Malvern High because she could fit it in around our school hours. Now I suspect she hasn't the confidence to apply for anything better. She's always telling me I have to do well at school so I don't end up with my hands down someone else's toilet.

The irony is, I would gladly clean toilets if it meant I could spend every moment of my spare time drawing and painting. Mum won't even let me take Art at high school. She says it can only ever be a hobby and I've lost track of how often she's called it a total waste of time. Harsh.

An hour later, Bailey calls out, "Come and check out your mum's haircut, J.D.!"

I stroll back into our small kitchen. I'm not sure what I expect. What I do *not* expect to see is my somewhat dowdy mother transformed into a very trendy woman with a fashionably blonde bob. There is absolutely no doubt where Mad gets her stunning good looks from. Mum is only thirty-five, previously looked forty and now Bailey has just taken ten years off her.

She is all giggly.

I realise my jealousy levels are creeping up alarmingly,

approaching ten on the Richter scale.

"You like?" asks Mum, with a tremor of insecurity in her voice.

I know I could burst her bubble with just one word. I confess, a part of me is actually tempted and I hesitate. I'm aware she's looking across at me somewhat anxiously. I battle the green-eyed monster and finally win.

"I don't just like, Mum, I *LOVE!*"

She beams and looks younger still. Bailey turns his head abruptly away, but not before I see his eyes glisten. He doesn't want me to know he's on the verge of tears; it's becoming a habit. And there is something else I suspect he is hiding. I see it in the way his hand hovers briefly above Mum's shoulder. My heart sinks in surprise and all I can think is, *bugger...*

Atonement

"Atonement!" states Bailey clearly at school lunchtime two days later.

"What?" I reply, my mouth half-full of a salami roll. A welcome change from the usual ham and cheese sandwich. Mum is getting adventurous.

"I think we should call our graphic novel *Atonement*."

"Why?" As usual his thoughts have left me way behind.

"Because it just feels right, J.D."

"Nah. Doesn't make sense. Besides, isn't that the name of a movie that came out a few years ago?"

Bailey's face darkens and I can see his jawline going tense and rigid.

"Trust me on this, J.D. *Atonement* is the perfect title for my book."

"*Atonement* sucks. Doesn't it mean making amends? And what does Proton have to make amends for anyway? What's he done that's so wrong? And for the record, last I heard, it was OUR book."

I'm feeling particularly belligerent and disillusioned today. In fact, I have been ever since Mum's haircut. Okay — so I could still be wrong about my deductions. I may have totally misread the whole situation and jumped to wild conclusions. But I don't think so. I idly wonder if Mum has guessed too. Then I dismiss the notion altogether. *Nah... she'll be clueless.*

Now I can see a vein throbbing in his temple and his fists are clenched. I realise I feel afraid of him; or perhaps it's just the strength and depth of his emotions I'm actually afraid of. I am also aware that although he is only fifteen, he has the physical body of a man.

Out of the corner of my eye I can see my form teacher, Mr Shields, looking across at us on the other side of the playground. Bailey's stance must appear quite threatening. Bailey has seen him too and takes a deep breath. He deliberately relaxes his fists.

Finally, he looks at me and says, "It was all his fault. Proton caused the death of his family and the destruction of his whole planet."

"Eh? I don't get it. I thought it was the people of Kane. Aren't they the bad guys?"

He gives a humourless laugh. "It's a metaphor, J.D. We all have Cain and Abel inside us."

"We do?"

"Of course. Darkness and despair versus light and hope; monsters versus gods... Each battling for supremacy and the control of our mind, body and spirit. Ever heard of that old Cherokee story of the two wolves?"

I am lost but decide to play along.

"Nope."

"An old Cherokee is talking to his grandson and explains about the terrible fight taking place inside himself, like two wolves. The black wolf is full of anger, jealousy, sorrow, self-pity, guilt, regret, lies and ego. The white wolf is full of joy, peace, love, hope, humility, kindness, truth, and compassion. He tells his grandson that the same battle is taking place in everyone."

"Who wins?"

Bailey chuckles. "That's exactly what the grandson asks."

"Well?"

"There are two versions of the story. In the first version, the grandfather simply replies: 'The one you feed.'"

"I like that. What about the second version?"

"Ah. Now this is my personal favourite. In the second version, he replies: 'If you feed them right, they both win.'"

"I don't get it."

"The black wolf also has qualities such as tenacity, courage and fearlessness that the white wolf lacks. The white wolf is full of caring and empathy and knows what is in everyone's best interests. Neither can be starved to death; their battle is eternal. They need each other. Feed them both and the internal struggle will end."

"I like that too. But how will Proton atone for his sins?"

"He is a superhero, so naturally he will perform good deeds and rescue people on earth."

"Naturally." Then another thought occurs to me. "Who will rescue Proton? Who protects the Protector?"

Bailey smiles, "*Atonement* means to make amends and do penance, but it has a much older meaning. It used to literally mean: AT-ONE-MENT."

"So?"

"So, when each of the wolves inside Proton are fed; equally respected, acknowledged and accepted — he will find internal peace and be at one with himself."

I notice the vein has stopped throbbing in his temple. Any fear I had felt has dissipated. I shrug my shoulders and say, "I still believe even superheroes need support sometimes; every Clark Kent needs a Lois Lane. But *Atonement* it is, then. Just don't blame me when some movie company buys the film rights to our book and complains the title has already been used."

He throws back his head and gives a throaty laugh.

All trace of the black wolf has gone.

Missing Link

The following Wednesday I have to stay after school for a three-way conference. Mad has hers first, while I wait on the bench outside. Then Bailey materialises with a grey-haired guy in tow. The man appears to be in his late fifties and looks uncomfortably nervous in an ill-fitting suit.

"J.D., I'd like you to meet my father, Adam. Dad, this is J.D."

I have to confess, Adam Summer is not exactly what I was expecting. For starters, he is considerably shorter than his son, plus, he has shifty bloodshot eyes that refuse to meet my own. Worse still, he positively reeks of alcohol.

I put out my hand to shake his. For a few seconds it honestly

feels like I'm holding onto a damp limp fish. I quickly release his hand and resist the urge to shudder.

As his father goes on ahead, Bailey hangs back and says, "What do you think of my old man?"

"Er... very pleasant."

He grins. "Actually, I picked the guy up outside the City Mission and hired him for an hour for a bottle of cheap plonk."

"You are joking, right?' I ask in undisguised horror.

Bailey gives me a carefully considered look and then laughs out loud, "Course I am. Had you going there for a moment!"

To be honest, I'm really not sure what to believe. Is Adam Summer a professional actor who has totally gone to seed, or is he just a local wino lured by yet another bottle? I am still trying to make up my mind when Mum and Mad reappear further down the corridor. Mad is wearing her usual slightly superior smug expression and Mum can't hide the obvious pride she is feeling. Sickening.

Then Mr Shields finally calls out my name and Mum and I enter the classroom just as Bailey and his dad leave. Bailey's eyes meet mine and they are dancing with amusement; I see him put out an arm to support Adam Summer as the older man stumbles.

Things do not bode well for my own three-way conference. Sitting on the desk immediately in front of Mr Shields is the start of Bailey's and my graphic novel. I have no idea how he has got hold of a copy, though I have a horrible suspicion Bailey had something to do with it. Mum will go totally ape-shit when she realises how much time I've wasted on it, especially when she finds out I haven't got one merit or excellence grade all term.

"Ah, Mrs Dawson. Delighted to see you again. *Delighted.* In fact, I almost didn't recognize you! Both you and Jane have obviously been to a wonderful stylist. *Wonderful.*"

Mum blushes in confusion. I smile and say, "Yes, Anthony at Servilles is certainly wonderful."

Mum glares at me.

"Well, I must say, Mrs Dawson, you look very becoming. *Very becoming.*"

Oh God. I think old Mr Shields is actually hitting on my mum...

Mum gently guides him back to reality. "Mr Shields, I am concerned about Jane's grades. Next year she starts her NCEA's."

"Indeed, *indeed.*" His repetition is also really starting to get to me.

"So what do you suggest? Extra homework? I'm afraid a tutor is out of the question."

Thank God for that.

"Ah. Well — actually, Mrs Dawson, it has recently been brought to my attention her astonishing skills and creativity in Art. *Astonishing.*" He points to Bailey's and my novel which now has the title **ATONEMENT** scrawled across the front in a loud graffiti style font.

"What I suggest is that Jane take up art and graphic design to replace subjects like business studies where she clearly struggles and has little interest."

I sigh. He is wasting his breath. Mum picks up the manuscript and flips quickly through it. I see her frown and then she gets that familiar set look across her face. It's the same look she always wears whenever I have asked to take art or graphics at high school.

"I want both Jane and Madeleine to take subjects that will allow them to find secure jobs once they leave school. She can doodle in her spare time at home."

I cringe at her use of the *d* word.

"Are you aware, Mrs Dawson, that there are many employment opportunities in the Arts?"

"Humph! My ex-husband was— let's just say it was a constant struggle for him to generate enough income to support his family."

"I don't quite follow, Mrs Dawson."

"He was... an artist," she added reluctantly.

What? Was he? He *was?* Our father was an *artist?* On my birth certificate his occupation is simply listed as 'labourer'. How come she never told me this before? I think of that slightly intense 'arty-farty' look in that photo of him and Mad. The uncomfortable expression in Mum's eyes whenever I pick up a pencil...

"I understand your fears, Mrs Dawson," replies Mr Shields in his most reassuring tone. "But the world is constantly changing. *Constantly.* I'm confident that Jane's artistic ability, combined with a graphics course, would stand her in very good stead employment-wise. Perhaps Jane has something to say here. Jane?"

I am still trying to put into place this latest critical piece of my paternal inheritance; the crucial missing link in my genetic jigsaw. And Mr Shields is now trying to convince my mother that I could one day earn my living as an artist. I confess, right at this moment, I want to hug him, even if he *is* old and wrinkly.

"Mum, drawing and painting mean to me what your love of books meant to you when you were my age. They are my passion. Please, please, *PLEASE* let me take art and graphic design!"

There is a long silence. I hold my breath.

Doubt, fear and indecision etch the line between Mum's eyes in permanent marker.

My eyes are glued to hers.

She rubs the line with two of her fingers.

I deliberately don't blink; I just hold her gaze.

Unbelievably, her shoulders start to slump.

Yeees!

"Okay, okay — I know when I'm outnumbered. Bailey even had a go at me the other day too. But I *do* expect a marked improvement in your other subjects, Jane, particularly maths."

I have a sudden mental image of the front of this morning's *Herald*. It showed a photo of a toddler who had somehow climbed inside one of those arcade claw games and physically grabbed the toy he had been unable to capture with the claw. The kid's mother looked seriously stressed, hands pressed frantically on the glass windows. But the little kid inside looked ecstatic.

Right at this moment, I feel just like that toddler and poor Mum is on the outside, looking in.

"She finally tells me after fourteen years." I complain to Bailey on the way to school the following morning.

"Great you can take art and graphics," he sidesteps.

"Fourteen years! Never realised I had any connection to the guy apart from a teaspoon of sperm."

"And now?"

"I know he's an artist. It explains *everything*."

Bailey frowns, "It does?"

"Duh! For starters, it explains why I'm good at art. It explains why Mum freaks out every time I touch a pencil. And why he buggered off."

"It does?" Bailey repeats.

His repetition reminds me of Mr Shields.

"Yeah. He must have buggered off because he had to fulfil his destiny as a painter and starve in a garret somewhere, probably Paris, and paint haunting images of prostitutes or something. Or maybe he's in New York and drips splatters of paint from a scaffold and is terribly misunderstood and—"

"Drew the Dripper," he laughs, remembering how I'd told him earlier my father's name is Andrew Dawson.

I glare at Bailey and stick out my tongue.

He ignores the gesture and adds, "Or maybe he's still in New Zealand. Ever thought of tracking him down?"

"Nope. The guy is still an arsehole: he ran out on Mum when she was pregnant with me, and Mad was just a toddler. Besides, I have the attitude that you can't miss what you've never had."

Bailey looks unconvinced.

It's now lunchtime and we are sitting on our usual bench.

"Bailey, do you believe in fate?"

He hesitates a moment and then says, "Sort of." It sounds more like 'Or ov' as his mouth is full of my chicken and mayo sandwiches. Actually, they are really Mad's — she is still sticking to her new-fad diet with religious fanaticism.

I try to keep Bailey on track. "I was looking for a simple *yes* or *no* answer here."

He laughs. "Fate is never simple, J.D. Yes, I do believe in it, but I also believe we can help it along."

"Give me an example."

"Well, take the day we first met and —"

"You mean the day you appeared in my kitchen doorway wearing that grey trenchcoat and looking just like my drawing of a superhero?"

"No. I mean three days earlier when you were running round a corner and crashed into me outside the Pakuranga Shopping Mall. I bent down and picked up your school books."

I gasp in surprise. "That was *you*?"

"Of course. Subconsciously I must have made quite an impact. Pun intended. I guess that's why you did the drawing."

I sit here, feeling stunned. I'd totally forgotten about that incident. I do remember it now — almost like a dream; fuzzy around the edges. I was racing to meet a girlfriend after school and collided with a hunky grey apparition. It was almost like he had stepped directly into my path. *So that was Bailey!*

Finally, I state, "But it was fate that you ended up moving in three doors down."

"Was it? Your name was written clearly on all your books. I could have tracked you down in the phone book."

"Our number is unlisted."

"Or followed you home."

I feel uneasy and swallow. "Bailey, now you are starting to creep me out."

He smiles gently. "Sorry, J.D. I'm a terrible tease. Here, I will give you a better example. I believe your mum is fated to pack in her cleaning job and get a fulfilling one as a librarian. But in order for fate to play its hand, she needs to know about the job in the first place. And she will need encouragement." Then he puts a piece of folded paper into my hand and abruptly takes off, just as the bell rings.

I open up the bit of paper: It's an advert for a full-time assistant librarian at Malvern High School — *experience preferred but not essential and must have a passion for books.* Now I get where he is coming from. But I still feel seriously creeped out.

I had no idea helping fate along could be such hard work. Prior to her job interview, Mum kept alternating between excitement and despair. She needed constant bolstering to offset her zero lack of self-confidence and in the end, Mad and I had to practically drag her along to the interview.

Then she made it to the shortlist and started biting her nails. Mad does that too when she's anxious before an exam.

"I'm sure I won't get it, girls. I mean, look at me! I'm far too old... and they will naturally want someone with qualifications."

Eventually, the school principal himself rang Mum to say he had good news and bad news. The good news: *Congratulations!* — she's got the assistant librarian position. The bad news: now they have to advertise for a new cleaner. I don't think I've seen her this happy in years. I send Bailey a text message and he replies: *It was fate LOL*

Personally, I think it was Bailey. He is a superhero to me and Mum. Mad doesn't need one, after all, she's always been spoilt with good looks and brains.

Drew the Dripper

Mum loves her new job. In the mornings I can even hear her humming away to herself. That *never* used to happen.

I know it's a cliché but it's like someone has switched a light on inside her; she's almost glowing with happiness. I guess she's finally living and not just going through the motions. And she's always bringing home books from the school library, reading whenever she's got a spare moment. She reads at the meal table, in front of the T.V., in bed and on the loo. The latter habit drives me nuts — we only have one loo.

Mum says she has to do this much reading so she can make

informed recommendations to students at school. Personally, I think she's just making up for lost time. She's a walking advert for that old saying: make your vocation your vacation.

Unfortunately, the honeymoon doesn't last. This week I've got the 'old mum' back again. Her internal light has gone out and I'm hoping it's just a temporary glitch; a momentary power cut.

Needless to say, I'm keeping a very low profile, getting to school on time, doing all my homework and helping out with dishes without being asked. But the atmosphere is seriously toxic. I'm not sure what else I can do.

On Sunday, Bailey whispers: "Whatsup with your mum?"

"Mega-case of stress," I whisper back.

Mum is crashing pots and pans together in the kitchen and hopefully can't hear us.

"Uh? Is it the new job? I thought she was happy in it."

"It's nothing to do with the library job — Mum adores it. But on Monday our car died and it's terminal; so we all have to catch the school bus. Even Mum... *embarrassing!* On Wednesday Mad accidentally downloaded a virus onto our one and only computer and there's no money to fix it, so now the screen is covered in crazy pop-ups. Thursday, Tripod got an abscess the size of a number eight egg after being picked on by a stray tom — so he's on a course of antibiotics and helping to pay off the vet's home loan. And yesterday our landlord threatened to give us ninety days' notice and turf us out of *our* home, as he's thinking of putting the house on the market."

"Shitarama! Anything I can do to help?"

"Not unless you're prepared to rob a bank."

The following Saturday Bailey insists on shouting us all afternoon tea in the City. He arranges to meet me, Mum and Mad in Vulcan Lane at three o'clock.

I know Bailey well enough by now to know he has an ulterior motive. I just can't figure it out. He says he wants to thank us all for making him feel so welcome in the neighbourhood... *Yeah, right.*

So I sit here and drink a hot chocolate and happily demolish a sizable portion of carrot cake. There are walnuts on the thick creamy icing and I savour every mouthful. Mad abstains apart from a diluted apple juice (Mad by name, mad by nature) and Mum and Bailey both have Earl Grey tea and blueberry muffins. Bailey seems his usual relaxed self, apart from a fleeting look of frustration when Mum pours a second cup of Earl Grey from the pot. That's when I know for sure he has his own agenda.

Eventually we exit the café and there, right opposite, is a flashy art gallery. Predictably, I want to check it out. Mad groans but Bailey propels her through the doorway after me. Mum follows, glancing at her watch, (she has a new book on the go and it's a page turner).

The main room is devoted to a menagerie of New Zealand artists. To be honest, a lot of the stuff I don't really get. Or maybe it's the setting that doesn't gel; a mish-mash of images competing for our attention in a clinical white windowless room that has about as much appeal as a public hospital. I feel momentary disappointment.

Off the main room is a smaller room with an arched floor to ceiling window at one end. It has a welcoming light airy feel and I escape into it. Opposite the window is a whole wall of paintings by an Australian artist. At least the little printed notice I'm staring at says he's an Aussie.

Funnily enough, it's Mad who notices the artist's name first. She and Mum have entered the room close behind me, and now she's looking over my shoulder.

"Hey," she says. "Check this out. This guy's surname is Dawson. Maybe he's a long lost rellie?"

She's joking.

I peer and see the first initial. It's an *A*. I glare across at Bailey who is making an unsuccessful attempt to look innocent.

I sidle over to him and hiss, "This was a set-up."

He smiles benignly. "So what do you think? Not a drip or a prostitute in sight..."

"The *A* could stand for Alex or Arron or—"

"Andrew. It's definitely Andrew. I checked."

"Of course you did." I gave him another glare.

He keeps smiling.

Finally, I look at the paintings. My father's paintings. Grudgingly, I have to admit they are good. In fact, they are better than good and going by all the red stickers, other people think so too.

I once read somewhere that art is 'not what you put in, it's what you leave out'. My father has that totally sussed. In one work he has taken a run-down building, zeroed in on a single broken window and then focused all his attention on painting the wrought iron bed end that is visible in one corner.

His images have a haunting stillness about them. He is the

sort of artist that would ignore a spectacular view in favour of painting an upturned twenty-four-gallon drum spilling over with rubbish: Australia's answer to America's Andrew Wyeth.

I watch Mum peering intently at the price labels that are printed directly under the name Andrew Dawson. Even the smallest sketches are over $5,000. I wonder if she has twigged yet that this artist is the same guy who left her to provide for a toddler, while I was busy forming fingers and toes inside her womb. So much for starving in a garret. Looks like we were the ones who repeatedly opened the door on an empty fridge.

I watch as Mum's mouth sets in a hard, uncompromising line. *Yep, she's twigged.*

The gallery assistant makes a b-line for Mum. She's all smiles, gold jewellery and red lipstick and I take a step back to avoid the sickly barrage of perfume and hairspray.

"I see you are admiring Andrew Dawson's exhibition," she gushes. "His work is bought by collectors all over the world you know. Americans just *LOVE* his paintings — they can't get enough of them."

She sweeps her eyes over Mum, obviously trying to decide if she is a potential customer. Mum's Warehouse jacket and pseudo leather shoes are a dead giveaway — the assistant is already poised on one heel and about to turn away and prey on another customer when Mum casually comments, "Actually, I already have two of his creations."

The assistant raises a surprised eyebrow. "You obviously collected them before his prices skyrocketed."

"Pardon me?" Mum's mouth has flat-lined.

Oops. Never a good sign.

"I only meant his work is probably out of your league. Not that I'm implying anything personal — you know, about your appearance — I mean, your financial situation..." The assistant is starting to perspire and appears a little desperate. She looks around for an escape route.

Mum blocks her path.

"I have two of Andrew Dawson's finest creations sharing my home in Pakuranga," states Mum. "They are both stunning examples of his early work."

Out of the corner of my eye I see Bailey whisper something to Mad. Her eyes widen. Now we are all hanging on to Mum's every word. Only the gallery assistant is unaware the conversation is no longer about art.

"I hope you have adequate insurance cover," says the assistant. "Prices have trebled, you know. This exhibition is the first major retrospective of his work in the Southern Hemisphere. I would *LOVE* to see photos of those early creations of Andrew's. Perhaps you could email them to—"

"Hang on," I interrupt. "Did you just say this was a retrospective exhibition?"

"Yes. A tragic business. Such a darling! He lived tax-free on Norfolk Island for the past ten years. Car accident. No street lights. Large cow on the road. Enormous estate. Reclusive. No family. His solicitors are in the process of trying to track down any surviving relatives. Everything could end up being left to charity and—"

Mum suddenly interrupts her barrage and says, "Personally,

I have always believed charity should begin at home." She smiles pleasantly but I can tell her brain is working overtime. She adds, "No need for me to email you those photos. I can introduce you to those two creations right now." Mum reaches out to Mad and me, pulling us over by our sweatshirts. We stand awkwardly on either side of her.

The gallery assistant stares back at us blankly.

"This is Madeleine," says Mum, "And this is Jane — Andrew Dawson's two daughters. I have birth certificates to prove it. Now, perhaps you would be so kind as to email me the name and address of Andrew's solicitor."

Bombshell

Bailey drops a bombshell one week later, immediately after Sunday roast.

"Are you aware, Laura, that Madeleine is suffering from a serious eating disorder?"

"What?" we both yell out in unison. Mad has just left the table and disappeared down the corridor.

"In fact," continues Bailey, "at this precise moment, she probably has her fingers down her throat and is throwing up in the bathroom sink."

Mum stands up abruptly and marches towards the bathroom. She is clearly a woman on a mission.

I look at Bailey, roll my eyes, and say, "You have really lost the plot this time."

He just shrugs and gives me a kind of sad, knowing smile.

He was right, of course. I am ashamed to say that, despite living in the same house as my sister and even sharing the same bedroom, I never even twigged anything was wrong. Mum feels even worse than me.

She tells me afterwards that when she'd burst into the bathroom, Mad was standing naked on the scales. Mum says she could smell sick in the air, so Bailey had been right, but what shocked Mum even more was seeing her beautiful daughter reduced to a skeletal figure. Mad resembled a victim from Belsen — one of those horrifying Nazi concentration camps we learn about in History.

It all makes sense to me now: how Mad always gets changed in the bathroom and never in our bedroom; the way she hides her body in baggy tracksuits and jettisons her lunch into my lunchbox; her obsessive running even when there are no specific events to train for.

Mad used to weigh sixty-five kilos and now she's just under forty. Mum says the extreme weight loss and throwing up has even affected the enamel on Mad's teeth and she has also lost her periods. Apparently, she can't look at food without seeing calories and she still believes she's fat. That's mental!

Our family doctor tells Mum that Mad will have to be hospitalised if she loses any more weight. He says she is suffering from a condition called 'anorexia nervosa' and it could ultimately affect her internal organs — her heart or kidneys — and kill her. That's serious shit.

Suddenly Mad's rapidly approaching NCEA's don't seem such a big deal anymore. Mum insists she puts them off till next year and just focuses on getting physically well. Even the school principal agrees. And Mad has to have weekly counselling sessions. Imagine that: having to go to a shrink when you are only sixteen.

The funny thing is, Mad doesn't make a real fuss about it. It's like the stuffing has been totally knocked out of her. And then, get this — out of the blue she asks if she can try out for a part in the end of year musical. We had no idea she had any interest in drama, let alone music.

The doctor says anorexia is as much a psychological illness as it is a physical one. With Mad's sudden interest in drama and singing, I wonder if she's now in lalaland. And I'm not talking about the movie.

Bailey disagrees. "Madeleine has been under enormous pressure to conform and meet other people's expectations. Remove those and she is suddenly free to pursue her passions. Out of interest — does your big sis like to sing in the shower?"

"Yeah, I guess so. But that doesn't really mean anything, surely? And why the need to deliberately starve herself?"

"I suspect it's a desire to have control in a world where she felt she had none. While a diet can be an attempt to control weight; anorexia is often an attempt to gain control over one's life and emotions. Besides, Madeleine is a perfectionist; she can't even go on a diet without taking it to its logical extreme."

"Bailey, I know she's my sister but I don't know what to say to her about all this stuff. I'm no therapist."

"Who says you need to even say anything? Maybe you just need to let her know you support her and will always be there to listen when she's ready to talk. Give her spontaneous hugs. Show her you love her, just the way she is."

I rest my hand lightly on his and ask, "How come you are always so wise?"

He pushes my hand away and mutters, "Put it down to personal experience."

I take one look at his face and realise the black wolf has just gained the upper hand.

Mad is sitting on the end of my bed. Her cheekbones are so prominent they look like they belong on an anime figure. How come I never noticed that till now? She's eating an apple. And I don't mean like you'd normally eat one. Her apple is cut up into neat little segments, carefully arranged in a bowl, and there are an exact equal number of tiny cubes of cheese.

She places a piece of cheese on an apple segment, pops it slowly into her mouth and chews even more slowly — if that's even possible. Bizarre. I think this must be part of her illness. I refrain from making my usual sarcastic comments.

I sidle over and give her an awkward hug. I can feel her whole rib cage protruding through the thin cotton of her turquoise t-shirt, a freebie from the local health food store. Ironically, its dayglo pink caption reads: *You Are What You Eat.*

"You okay?" I ask inanely.

She shrugs, "No... but I think in time I will be."

"Are you mad at Bailey for guessing and telling Mum?"

She frowns. "He's a strange guy, Jane, but for some reason I trust him to look out for us all... and he did the right thing telling Mum. A part of me knows I'm not well. I get dizzy climbing even the smallest flight of stairs, and I feel cold all the time lately."

I glance down at her arms and notice her goosebumps. I reach over for my dressing-gown and put it around her shoulders. The smile she gives me is shaky and vulnerable.

"What gets me," I say softly, "is that Bailey noticed your weight loss and I didn't. I feel really stink about that. Don't laugh, but deep down I think of him as our personal superhero."

She looks at me through eyes that now appear far too large.

"Try not to get too attached to him, Jane."

"What do you mean?"

"The Petersons are due back from their cruise beginning of December. Bailey will probably move out of the neighbourhood then."

"His parents might buy a place in the same school zone."

Mad looks doubtful and says, "Mmm." She picks at a loose thread on the patchwork bedspread, then blurts out, "Do you want to know what I really think?"

"Spill."

"I think your friend Bailey is a squatter and his parents don't even exist."

I stare back at her, stunned.

Mark of Kane

Ever since Mad put the idea out there, I have a horrible suspicion she is spot on. It all makes sense. Why I've never yet seen Bailey's mum or dad pulling in or out of the Petersons' driveway; that awful wino Bailey passed off as his father at the three-way-conference; and then, of course, there is his constant desire for food as if no one is at home to feed him.

At school today I am deliberately sneaky.

"Bailey, Mad was wondering if you could introduce her to your parents. Them being in the theatre and all and now that she's got a role in *Godspell*."

"Wow, she's in *Godspell* — that's amazing! Who's she playing?"

"Mary Magdalene." I'm not easily distracted and add, "So — can she meet your folks sometime?"

"Um, yeah, sure thing, J.D."

I confess I am more than a little relieved.

Seconds later he adds, "Unfortunately, they are both really tied up with a big production at the moment. They won't be free for at least three weeks."

The Petersons return in three weeks.

Oh God, Mad could be right...

Bailey is producing storyboards for our graphic novel at an alarming pace. I am having trouble keeping up. In the story, Proton moves from one small town to the next, stumbling upon families in need of rescue: sometimes from greedy land developers; sometimes from hoons on the rampage. Another time he saves an innocent girl about to be attacked by an evil being.

"Is it a human or a monster?" I ask Bailey.

"Monsters don't exist," he replies. "But human beings are capable of doing and saying monstrous things."

I notice his mouth is set in concrete. In fact, his whole body has gone suddenly rigid, as if he's just looked into the face of Medusa. It's hard to tell if he's feeling hurt or angry. I suspect both.

I let him cool off and idly flick through the new storyboards. Always in the background there are the people of Kane, appearing in darkened alleyways, tailing Proton's car, hunting him down. In all my previous illustrations, I've depicted them as indistinct, shadowy figures glimpsed out of the corner of one's eye. But now they are closing in on Proton and I'm not sure how to depict them in any detail. I glance across at Bailey; he seems calm once again.

"Bailey, you've never told me what they actually look like."

"Who?"

"The people of Kane."

"Ah… they always wear suits."

"I know *that*. What else?"

"Well, they tend to be very narrowminded."

Hello! How exactly am I supposed to depict narrowmindedness?

"What about 'the mark of Kane' you talked about initially?"

"It's invisible."

"Brilliant. And how can I draw an invisible mark?"

"I mean it's invisible to human eyes. Proton has super vision, remember? He can kill with just one look or he can render the invisible, visible by altering his focus."

"So what does the mark of Kane look like through Proton's super vision?"

This is as slow and painful as a tooth extraction.

"Actually, J.D., I have absolutely no idea. I am but a mere mortal! Even in the bible, there is no clear consensus as to what the mark of Cain actually was. The word translated as *mark* in Genesis could mean a sign, an omen, a warning, a gesture or even a Hebrew letter on his cheek. When Cain spilt his brother's blood, the earth became cursed as soon as the blood hit the ground. Should Cain attempt to farm the land, it would not produce a yield for him. He was forced to become a fugitive and a wanderer."

"God, Bailey Summer, you're infuriating sometimes. I don't recall signing up for a bible class."

"Aww... come on, admit it, J.D. You love me, really." He's thawed out now and his tone is playful.

I realise at this moment, I truly do. I love Bailey. I love the way he can make me laugh and cry all in the space of two minutes. I love the way his eyes crinkle up just before he gives his lopsided grin. And the way he unconsciously pokes the tip of his tongue out when he is writing and deep in concentration. Most of all, I love how he has seen through all of us, me, Mum and Mad and rendered the invisible, visible.

I incline my head and whisper, "Perhaps I do... even if you *are* a compulsive liar."

He starts to redden. "What's that supposed to mean?"

For once I have caught him off balance. Now is the moment to challenge him about his parents. Ask him if he is actually squatting at the Petersons'. But I don't. Instead I say, "I believe you know *exactly* what the mark of Kane looks like."

He gives a relieved chuckle. "Clever girl, now you've caught me out! The mark of Kane is a small irregular pockmark just above the left eyebrow."

His skin changes back to its normal tone, but I think he knows that wasn't what I meant to say. And there's other stuff I never even dared to voice: *if he is a squatter doomed to wander, exactly whose blood did he spill?*

Internet Dating

"Mad, what's the difference between loving someone and being *in* love?"

Mad sits there on her bed and stops humming. She's been humming the same tune all morning; the one called *By My Side* from that musical she's in. She's still painfully thin, with bones protruding. Even more noticeable now since she stopped covering herself up under baggy clothes and is currently wearing skinny jeans. But she hasn't lost any more weight — Mum checks every day on the bathroom scales.

"Mm..." says Mad, "that's a tricky one. I think when you love someone, you feel all warm inside when you think about them. When you are *in* love, that person can also make your toes curl up."

Last year Mad dated Rory Clark for several months — all blond hair and bulging muscles but no one exactly home up-top, if you get what I mean. I think Mad fell for him really hard. At least until she discovered he was two-timing with Lucy Braithwaite — a stick-figure who serves pies in the school tuck-shop (that's an oxymoron). Anyway, I'm pretty sure Rory must have made Mad's toes curl. Lucy's too by the sound of things.

I try to remember if my toes have ever curled up around Bailey. I don't believe they have, but I do get a hollow feeling in the pit of my stomach whenever I think of losing him. I guess that's why I never challenged him about the lies. I'm afraid I'll drive him away and lose the little bit of time we have left together.

Mad and I talk constantly now. It's as if by realising she is fragile and vulnerable, I can finally open up and feel close to her. And because I'm spilling my guts out, I guess she now feels free to do the same. But mostly we just natter about nothing in particular. Sister stuff.

Something just occurs to me. "Did you go on a diet because of Lucy Braithwaite?"

"Yeah. She called me a fat cow."

"Bitch. She's a stick insect. She'll probably chew Rory's head off if they ever mate and it'll serve him right."

Mad giggles. "That's what praying mantises do, not stick

insects. But I appreciate the thought."

"At least our dad wasn't two-timing Mum. Are you sad we never got a chance to meet him again?"

"Yeah, a little. But I think he was a better artist than he was a person. Mum says he gave her the best parts of himself through you and me."

I hug my knees and rock slowly back and forth. "Now that Mum's packed in the rest home job, she has spare time at last."

"Uh-huh."

"And she looks so attractive since Bailey cut her hair — it seems such a waste..."

"Where are you going with this?"

I grin. "I think Mum needs to find some romance in her life."

Mad rolls her eyes, "And what *exactly* are you proposing here?"

"Internet dating, of course!"

When I tell Bailey about my bright idea, he is unimpressed.

"Listen, J.D., there are a hell of a lot of dodgy men out there who can pretend to be one thing when they are really another."

Well, that's certainly rich coming from you, I think, but all I reply is, "I want to give fate a helping hand."

"Yeah right. Just don't cry on my shoulder when it all goes pear-shaped."

"So will you help me?"

"Sorry, J.D. You're on your own with this one. I don't believe in interfering in other people's love lives."

I give him a sulky look and mutter, "Killjoy."

He laughs and starts to walk away.

Infuriated, I yell after him, "Passion killer!"

He half-turns and blows me a kiss.

I feel its warmth, even across the playground, but a part of me wonders why Bailey is so dead against the idea. What if I misread that whole business when he cut Mum's hair? What if Bailey... *Eww!* Surely he doesn't fancy... nah, that's just plain nuts.

Though all the more reason to plug internet dating, just in case.

"You two *are* joking, right?" says Mum, when Mad and I first suggest the idea.

When Mum realises we are serious, she is initially appalled. Then Mad shows her some of the sites available and points out that Sue Knox, the office lady at Malvern High School, had met her partner that way.

"You mean Phillip? Goodness, who'd have thought. And he's such a lovely man."

Okay, so it wasn't easy, but after a week of wearing her down, Mum finally relents and registers with the same site Sue had told her she'd used.

The first guy she met for lunch in the City was pretty awful. He was a builder and, according to Mad, he had asked Mum on the very first date, "Are all your needs satisfied?"

She replied, "Yes, thank you. I am a great believer in DIY."

Guy number two was in advertising and a very smooth operator. He lasted three dates before Mum saw through the charm and sensed the rot in the middle.

"Are you sure you're not just getting picky?" I ask her after she'd dumped him.

"Trust me, Jane. When it comes to men, it pays to be picky. Unfortunately, when you reach my age, men are like parking places outside a busy supermarket."

"I don't get it."

Mad does though. "What Mum is trying to say, in a very politically incorrect way, is that the only ones available are the 'disabled' ones."

I still look at them both blankly.

Mum sighs and spells it out for me. "The older we get, the more emotional baggage we acquire and the more flawed we can become as human beings."

"Now I get it! So only the most damaged guys are available." Somehow, this does not bode well.

After four more unsuccessful dates, Mum finally reaches the point where she is going to give up on the whole idea. Then I persuade her to try one more. Call it instinct or gut feeling, but something about this latest guy's profile resounds in me at a very deep level.

"I don't know, Jane. He's a widower. He will always be comparing me to his dead wife. It's hard to compete with a dead woman."

"At least he didn't divorce his last four wives like that awful travelling salesman you had dinner with on Saturday."

"True."

"And it says here he's a policeman. Look on the bright side:

he won't be growing marijuana in his vegetable patch like guy Number Four." We have reached the point where we call them by number. The policeman will be Number Seven.

Mum eventually agrees to meet Number Seven in Devonport. It's supposed to be a lunch date but she doesn't get home until 9.30 p.m.

Both Mad and I pounce on her as she walks in the door.

"Where were you?" I ask.

Mad talks over me, "We've been worried sick!"

Mum gives us a slightly bemused look. "Girls, I think we have a serious case of role reversal here." She brushes past us and goes through to the lounge.

Mad follows, and I see them exchange quiet words (Mum still excludes me from stuff she thinks I'm too young to hear).

So frustrating!

"Well?" I ask Mad afterwards.

She grins and whispers, "I think Number Seven makes her toes curl."

When Mum tells us he looks like Sean Connery, it's inevitable we rename her latest guy '007'. We still haven't met him yet, but I can tell Mum is smitten. I can't wait to brag to Bailey that this dating lark has finally been a success.

I corner him at lunchtime. "Mum's been out with 007 twice since the weekend."

"Mm…"

He is switching me off again. He is busy working on yet

another storyboard and I guess it will be about the people of Kane. He is becoming obsessed with them appearing suddenly in their smart suits to relentlessly hunt Proton down. Then I casually mention 007 is a policeman and Bailey's head shoots up like a rocket.

"You didn't tell me he was a policeman!"

"Course I did, but you keep switching me off."

"Does he come to your house?" He is trying to sound casual, but he looks on edge.

"Nah. Mum doesn't want us to meet him yet. She says she wants to take things slowly and meet in a neutral environment."

Bailey visibly relaxes and then mutters, "She's very wise."

I wonder what he has done that makes Bailey so nervous of the police? Or perhaps he is simply afraid of being caught squatting at the Petersons'? They are due back next week. Maybe he really is a distant relation, I think hopefully. I am lying in bed, mulling over all these questions and give a sigh.

"You okay, Jane?" asks Mad. Her bed is on the opposite wall to mine. Neat and tidy compared to my train wreck.

"Yeah. Just worrying about Bailey and wondering what's going to happen next week."

"I told you not to get attached."

I sigh again and add, "Too late for that."

"Oh God, Jane — don't tell me you're in love with him!"

I can feel her waiting expectantly in the dark for my answer. I choose my words carefully.

"Mad, I think Bailey could be gay. It's not obvious of course, but I've seen the way he looks at Alistair Drummond, our new gym coach. And that certain way he holds his hands when he's talking... I first noticed it after he cut Mum's hair. Though, for one crazy moment recently, I did wonder if he had a crush on Mum."

She giggles. "Mum and Bailey? You silly sausage: that's not crazy — it's hilarious! And yes, he is definitely gay. He told me ages ago — that time at the meal-table. But I didn't feel I could betray a confidence."

So that's what he told her! I feel a bit miffed he hadn't confided in me first. But I can't really blame Mad for that. We are both silent for a while and then I finally admit, "I love Bailey as a soul mate. Does that make sense? When he leaves, I will feel like there is a part of me missing."

She nods her head gravely. "Love of a soul mate is the hardest love to lose."

"Why?"

"Because lovers come and go, but soul mates last forever."

Well, isn't that just brilliant.

I turn over and quietly reach out for Big Ted under the covers.

Dead End

The next day is a Saturday. Bailey sends me a text message to meet him at the bus stop at the top of the road. He also says predictably: *bring lunch* ☺

I raid the fridge and grab the fifty dollars I've saved up from odd garage sales. I stuff the food and money in a backpack along with a warm sweatshirt. It's December but it can still get chilly in the evenings. I don't know where we are going or what to expect, but I want to be prepared for anything.

The first bus that comes along has **Downtown** written across the front.

"Come on," says Bailey, "This one is ours."

I'm disappointed. A day in a noisy smog-filled city — Perfect — *Not!* Most of the bus ride I stare out the window, sulking. Sharing Bailey with half of Auckland City is not exactly high up there on my wish list. At Britomart we get off the bus, Bailey grabs my hand and he immediately leads me across the road to the old ferry building. We pool our money and he purchases two tickets. I'm a bit shocked to get so little change back. The next thing I know we are boarding the *Quickcat* ferry to Waiheke Island.

"Why Waiheke?" I ask Bailey.

"Why not?" he shrugs.

We sit outside on the very top deck and my sulky mood rapidly dissolves in the salt spray. Any remains are quickly blown away by the ocean breeze as the ferry picks up speed past Devonport. Bailey is silent but he looks relaxed — his long legs stretched out casually in front of him. It's an easy silence and I don't feel any need to fill it. The only time Bailey breaks it is to quietly point out a small pod of dolphins swimming off the port bow. At least that's what Bailey called it; 'left front' to a landlubber like me.

The ferry docks forty minutes later at Matiatia wharf — my first ever visit to the so-called 'Jewel in Auckland's Hauraki Gulf'. The tourists are quickly swallowed up by tour buses and taxis, and a steady stream of traffic shoots past us. In their wake I become aware of a sudden change of pace: traffic noise is replaced by a chorus of delicate bird song and the gentle repetitive buzz of cicadas. A hawk glides effortlessly along the skyline. We idle up the hill.

Instead of Oneroa and Onetangi, where most of the other tourists are heading in their overloaded double-deckers, we end up pottering down to Blackpool Beach. Bailey says the northern beaches are sandy with scatterings of delicate shells. In contrast, Blackpool is smothered in stones and seaweed and the only person we see is a middle-aged woman walking a boisterous collie along an adjacent road. It's a large dog with scruffy long hair and he looks like he should be named 'Rags' or 'Einstein'.

Local council signs dot the beach warning that dogs must be securely on leads at all times to protect the numerous seabirds. According to Bailey, the birds foraging delicately in the mudflats are mainly pied stilts and oystercatchers, but at certain times of the year he says it's also possible to get sightings of rare dotterels.

"But the really amazing birds that come to this particular beach annually are the godwits."

He points one out to me. To be honest, it looks pretty unimpressive. Nothing to get excited and jump up and down about.

"So what's so amazing about godwits?"

In typical Bailey fashion, he doesn't answer me directly. Instead, he says: "Kua kite te Kohanga kuaka?"

"Eh?"

"It's an old Maori riddle: *Who has seen the nest of the kuaka?* Kuaka is the Maori name for godwit."

"Now you've totally lost me, but I'm impressed. I didn't

know you could speak Maori."

He gives me a sheepish grin. " I can't. I've just read it all off this council sign. It says here that the riddle was only solved in 2007 when satellite-tagging traced the flight of godwits to Alaska — that's where their breeding grounds are. And why it was impossible for Maori to ever find their nests! Every year godwits return to New Zealand to feed and rest again. Some return to this same stretch of beach on Waiheke."

"So? Lots of birds migrate. I still don't get why they are that special."

"In September they fly direct from Alaska to New Zealand — an eleven thousand kilometre journey over the Pacific Ocean. They are a wading-bird and, unlike seabirds, they cannot rest on water or feed at sea. It's the longest non-stop flight undertaken by any bird on our planet."

"Jeez!"

"And when the poor buggers finally arrive on Waiheke," continues Bailey, "they are sometimes so weak they can barely stand or fold their wings properly."

I look across at the godwit with renewed interest. It's still remarkably unimposing: mottled brownish-grey plumage, short legs and a long thin bill. But I shake my head in awe — now I get it! But I'm also keeping an anxious eye on that hyperactive collie.

Now don't get me wrong — I'm actually a dog lover. I'm the sort of person who says you can kill off anyone in a movie as long as the dog lives. The only reason we don't have a dog is because Mum says we can't afford another mouth to feed, plus

— our landlord would go totally apeshit. (He doesn't know about Tripod; cats are easier to hide).

I'm sure this particular canine is a couch potato at home, but right now I swear he has the vulnerable godwit in his direct line of sight; the black wolf itching to gain supremacy over the white. Imagine flying that enormous distance just to end up as a dog's entrée?

I know Bailey is watching too. His whole body has gone tense.

The owner suddenly yells out, "Yeti!"

The dog lopes towards her, his long scruffy hair flowing up and down in the breeze as he eagerly reaches out to swallow the tantalising treat she has just produced from a pouch around her waist. She secures him to a leash and he obediently walks to heel; the white wolf is fed and, momentarily, wins.

We spend the next few hours exploring caves and rock pools, skimming stones into the sparkling clear waters and working our way through the food in my backpack. I never fail to be amazed at how much Bailey can consume. I've decided his stomach is like a human garbage disposal unit. The sandwiches are mostly cucumber and pathetically soggy. Bailey doesn't seem to mind; it's a case of straight down the hatch.

At three o'clock he suddenly announces it's time to head back.

"Back where?"

"Home. Your mum will be getting worried otherwise."

"I thought—"

"What?"

"Nothing." In truth, I have no idea what I thought. I sense today is the end of something. Deep down I guess I'm in denial and want it to be the start of something instead.

I follow him up a side road. After ten minutes I say, "This isn't the way we came."

Bailey shrugs. "It's a short cut."

Then he makes an abrupt veer to the left, down a narrow dirt track enclosed on either side by dense bush. I hesitate under the road sign clearly marked 'DEAD END'.

"Bailey, this is a dead-end road."

He gives a humourless laugh and says, "It's a matter of perception, J.D. Some would argue that life itself is a dead-end road. We all have to die eventually, so why even bother going anywhere?"

I sense a definite downward spiral in his mood. His eyebrows are drawn together in a frown and now there is an uncomfortable intensity about his stride. I struggle to keep up and reluctantly follow his retreating frame down the narrow road. Strictly speaking, it's more of a wide rough track than a road. And although it's a late sunny afternoon, it appears much darker in the native bush, with pongas and black tree ferns lining our path; the leaves of large karakas stubbornly blocking out any stray ultraviolet rays.

After another five minutes I start to get even more uneasy. It feels like we are in the middle of the 'wop wops'; miles away from civilisation. I know Bailey well enough to know he has brought me here for a reason. Only problem is, I can't for the life of me figure it out. I keep thinking about his fear of the police... *what had they ever done to him?* I'll rephrase that: *what could he possibly have done to make him feel so afraid of them?* More importantly — *what is he capable of doing now?*

Bailey grabs my arm and I give a start. But he simply pulls me over to the side of the track and points up into a delicate pittosporum.

"Do you see it, J.D.?"

"See what?" I ask nervously.

"Keep looking."

Then I see a flit of movement and say, "All I can see is a tiny grey bird. It's smaller even than a sparrow."

"That's it! It's a grey warbler. Now listen..."

So I ignore my thumping heartbeat and the sound of my blood pumping in my ears. Finally I hear a beautiful bird call: almost like liquid music. I gasp.

Bailey smiles and says, "They look so tiny and insignificant, but grey warblers create one of my favourite sounds in the bush."

I finally relax then, and lean back against him. He puts his hands on my shoulders and his chin now rests lightly on the top of my head. Then the bird flies off, surprised by a pair of raucous tui who swoop down to taste the new flowers on a nearby flax bush.

Bailey squeezes my shoulders. "Come on, J.D. I'll race you to the end of the road!"

I laugh. Almost too loudly, but it carries all my relief. It feels as though the grey warbler has flown away with Bailey's moodiness. I start frantically running. He is gracious enough to give me a decent head start but he still sails past moments later, his long legs propelling him with ease down the rough track like a Marvel Comic superhero. I arrive at the end of the road puffing and panting, desperate for a long cool glass of water.

"Is there any water left in that drink bottle I packed this morning?" I ask hopefully, half doubled over, clutching a stitch that has formed deep in my stomach.

He shakes the orange plastic bottle, covered in embarrassingly old stickers of *Powerpuff Girls*. "Nah, sorry, J.D. But I know where we can easily refill it."

I straighten up and look around. We are surrounded by bush at the end of a dead-end road. It hasn't rained for at least three weeks, so even a bush stream would barely be running at this time of year.

I give Bailey a mocking look, "Yeah, right."

He grins and replies, "Follow me, ye of little faith." Then he leaves the track and takes off into the bush with only his white t-shirt indicating a trail for me to follow.

I hesitate and then run after him, ignoring my stitch. I realise I would follow Bailey anywhere. I've got a horrible feeling I'm just like those desperate females you read about in women's magazines. You know the sort: the ones who obsessively correspond with murderers in prison, convinced they are going to reform them, only to end up their next victim. I shake off my irrational qualms: *if Bailey fears the police, it must be for a good reason... after all, isn't he our very own personal superhero?*

Taniwha

We come to a deep ravine where massive sinkholes have been carved out by decades of persistent stormwater. Long thick ship's ropes, green with age, are hanging down from enormous branches. Bailey grabs hold of one and laughingly sails across the gully, yelling at the top of his lungs: "Ahhh...aaa...Ahhhh... aaa...Ahhhhhhhhhh!"

"Hang on, Tarzan! Wait for me!" I scream after him. My thirst and stitch are forgotten and I clutch on excitedly to the nearest rope. I feel like I'm nine years old again and Bailey is my older brother. We play together like that for ten minutes, swinging back and forth across the gully, sometimes misjudging the landing and getting our sneakers covered in mud. In the end, I get rope burn and stop. Bailey leaps off his rope and hunkers down by the trickling stream.

I watch as he bends forward and plunges his right hand into the muddy channel. Now his whole arm, up to his elbow, is drowning in the pungent slimy blackness. After several minutes he pulls out a thick snake about thirty centimetres long and holds it out to me.

I step back, instantly grossed out.

He laughs. "It's an eel. Haven't you ever seen an eel before? Here, touch it."

I swallow and shake my head. I really don't want to. To be honest, there is something uncomfortably phallic about it.

"Come on. Touch it!"

He thrusts it towards me, his manner almost aggressive now.

Just to shut him up, I reach out and touch the constantly twisting body of the eel with my fingertips. It feels smooth and powerful; pure muscle. Icky. I join in his laughter — but mine is higher pitched and nervous. It's as though this place is a minefield of triggers for Bailey and this eel is yet another one.

He returns the eel to the mud and the creature is abruptly swallowed up by gooey oblivion. Bailey stares at the place where the eel disappeared, as if his thoughts have followed down the same endless hole. I sense the black wolf has returned.

"That was just a young one," mutters Bailey. "Probably ten or twelve years old — only now will its sex be determined... it

can still become either male or female." He adds softly, "Can you imagine that?"

I choose this moment to quote a couple of 'Fun Facts' I read recently on the packaging of a sanitary pad: "Did you know the longfin eel can live a hundred years? And they can grow as long as two metres?"

He whispers, "So they end up like monsters; Taniwha,"

Bailey once told me that monsters didn't exist. I figure now is not a good time to point that out to him. Instead, I say, "I thought Taniwha were just a Maori myth?"

He shrugs, "Myths and legends nearly always have some basis in reality. You just have to know where to look."

Then Bailey shakes his head, almost like he's throwing off an imaginary Taniwha, and he grabs my hand with his clean left one. He goes to pull me up a steep bank. I'm perfectly capable of negotiating the bank by myself, but I like feeling his hand in mine, so I hold on tight. I become aware we are actually climbing steps, long since covered by wandering jew and wild lemon balm. The pungent smell of the balm teases my senses when squashed underfoot. As the steps end, Bailey leads me triumphantly through the canopy of bush into brilliant sunshine. I let go of his hand and realise, in surprise, we are now standing at the bottom of someone's suburban lawn, overgrown with daisies and sticky paspalum.

At the far end of the lawn stands a white two-storey weatherboard house with a garage alongside. The garage guttering is attached by a plastic downpipe to the largest wooden barrel I have ever seen in my entire life. Bailey strolls across the lawn to the water butt, turns a brass tap and proceeds to wash the caked mud off his right hand and arm. Then he fills our drink bottle.

He offers me the first swig, saying with a twinkle in his eye, "Nature's wine for Madam..." He pronounces it the French way so it sounds like *Madame* and he waves his arm in an elaborate flourish.

I giggle and drink greedily, delighted his mood has switched yet again. The delicious fresh rain-water is ice-cold and I feel it dribbling down my chin. Bailey reaches a hand across and wipes it away with the edge of his sweatshirt.

In between gulps I splutter, "Thanks!"

He gives that enigmatic smile of his and replies, "You're welcome." Then he refills the plastic bottle again for himself. As he drinks, I look across at the house.

It has a sad, abandoned look. Paint is peeling, green mould has darkened the weatherboards facing the south, and lichen smothers the corrugated iron roof. But it still oozes charm. There is a metal chimney on a precarious lean — probably attached to some sort of woodstove inside. There is even a turret with a shingle roof jutting out onto the back deck.

Mum once showed me a YouTube video of an old television programme she watched as a teenager called *The Waltons*. This is definitely a Waltons' style house and I can almost hear the ghostly echo of children playing in the garden on a summer's evening, calling out goodnight to each other, tired but happy...

"Come on, J.D. Time to go. It's already after four o'clock and we need to catch the five ferry back to town."

"Do you think anyone lives here?"

"Nah. It's just a holiday bach for the summer. A lot of places are like this on Waiheke. Abandoned for several months of the year."

On impulse, I step up onto the deck and peer through a window covered in cobwebs. Bailey seems on edge all of a sudden and hangs back. I ignore him and look through a crack in the drawn curtains. It appears to be a young girl's bedroom. There is a white wrought-iron bed, just like the one in that movie *Bedknobs and Broomsticks* only smaller, topped with a colourful patchwork quilt. A bookcase spills over with children's books and tween paperbacks and in one corner, on a low table, sits the most amazing dolls' house.

"Hey, Bailey. You ought to check this out! It's the most incredibly bizarre dolls' house I've ever seen. It's three storeys high with crooked steps, a crooked chimney, shingles and all the windows and doors are a funny shape and—"

"There was a crooked man who walked a crooked mile..." he whispered.

"And lived in a crooked house!" I exclaim in delight. Then I see his stricken white face. He suddenly looks much, much older. Like he's seen a ghost or is being haunted by one. I jump back down off the deck. I don't know what I've said or done to upset him. But I know it's time to leave.

"So which way to the ferry?" I say lightly, desperate to change his mood.

He looks away. He is trying to regain control of his emotions and when he finally speaks, his words sound harsh and mechanical. "We turn left out the front gate and follow the tar-seal. It's a thirty minute walk."

I suspect he has done this walk many times before. I wonder who exactly he has done it with.

We are both silent on the ferry trip back to the City. The silence continues while we wait for the next Howick and Eastern bus to draw up. On the ride to Pakuranga, Bailey suddenly hands me a wad of storyboards from his small backpack.

"It's the last chapter, J.D."

I stare at the pages blankly, tracing my fingers idly over his crude stick figures. Then I thrust them into my own pack and say, "Bailey, if I ask you some questions, will you answer me honestly?"

He hesitates.

Finally, he replies, "I'll try but only *yes* or *no* answers, okay?"

"Okay." My voice trembles slightly and I realise I'm suddenly afraid of the answers. I take a deep breath and then fire off the first one before I lose my nerve: "Is Bailey Summer your real name?"

"No."

"Did you ever live in Christchurch?"

"No."

"Are you related to the Petersons?"

"No."

"Was that man, Adam, really your father?"

I see a flash of Bailey's teeth. "No."

Finally I ask the question I have been putting off. "After

today, will I ever see you again?"

He smiles gently. "Why only ask the questions you know I shall answer *no* to?"

I frown and try to ignore the sick hollow feeling in the pit of my stomach. Then I say bluntly, "Are you gay?"

A long silence follows.

Eventually he gives a whispered, "Yes".

I swallow and say firmly, "I love you as a soul mate. Do you love me that way?"

He leans across and deliberately puts his lips against my forehead. His voice when he answers is deep and raspy, "One hundred percent YES!" Then he puts a finger under my chin and adds, "I need you to promise me something."

"What?"

"Keep a close eye on Madeleine. Anorexics are a bit like alcoholics. They will lie to hide their habit. She is not out of the woods yet and needs you to be strong for her. Don't go getting all maudlin over my absence."

I look at him slightly desperate. "What about our book?"

"It achieved what I intended it to achieve."

"I don't get it. I thought we were going to make a name for ourselves?"

He sighs and looks at me through grief-stricken eyes. "J.D. I wanted atonement for the terrible things I've caused. The book was simply a means to an end."

He reaches up, pulls the cord and the bus lurches to a halt. It's our stop. I step onto the kerb and turn back to ask him one more question. He isn't there. Confused, I spin around

— I suddenly realise he never got off the bus. He had never intended to.

The bus is already moving away and I run frantically after the cream and maroon vehicle, yelling out his name repeatedly.

"Bailey, stop! *Bailey!* **BAILEY!**"

As it turns the corner, I catch a glimpse of his face. He is deathly pale and I can see his handsome features all scrunched up. Then the bus roars away up the Pakuranga highway leaving black fumes in its wake. I know I've lost him. And I haven't even found out his real name.

Return of the Petersons

I walk through the kitchen doorway, tears streaming down from swollen eyes, only to find Mum out on another date with 007 and Mad sitting at the kitchen table with a plate in front of her. On the plate are tiny slivers of Kransky sausage with a small even square of cheese on each one.

"What's this?" I ask suspiciously, wiping my face on the sleeve of my sweatshirt.

"My dinner," she states weakly, avoiding my eyes.

Something snaps inside me. I march over to the fridge. Thankfully Mum's been to the supermarket since this morning.

I pull out a box of eggs, a block of Colby cheese, some button mushrooms and a large ham hock. I start to cut generous chunks off the hock.

"What are you doing?" she asks. I can practically see her salivating.

"I'm about to make us both an omelette. We can use your itsy-bitsy sausages as a garnish."

"I can't—"

"You can!" I yell fiercely. "I've just lost my soul mate and I'm damned if I'm going to lose my only sister as well." On impulse, I reach out and hug her. I am shocked that I can still feel all her ribs. I thought she was supposed to be putting on weight? She trembles, and for a few seconds she clings on to me. Right now Mad doesn't feel like my big sister.

"Here," I say, gently untangling myself. "You can beat the eggs."

Fifteen minutes later, she eats the generous omelette. I think we both know she has turned a corner.

Afterwards, she asks, "So Bailey's definitely gone?"

I nod my head pathetically and start to dissolve. Mad immediately pulls me into her arms. Suddenly I am the little sister again, and I bawl my eyes out.

I spot Mrs Peterson a week later outside Woolworths. She looks bronzed and relaxed.

"How was your cruise?" I ask.

"Fabulous, thanks Jane. Absolutely fabulous! We are already saving up for the next one. Asia next time. Perhaps Japan in the spring; all those stunning cherry blossoms."

"Sounds cool. Umm... Everything okay when you got home?"

"Yes and no. Keith wanted to report the whole business to the police."

"Business?" I say, trying to sound innocent.

"We think someone was living in our house while we were away. I know I should feel violated, but it's hard to, in the circumstances."

"I don't follow?"

"They left the place immaculate. Cleaned and fixed the broken gutter I've been on at Keith to do for ages. The back door no longer sticks. Two broken hinges in the bathroom cabinet were replaced. The oven, which I confess was filthy when we left, is now pristine. The outside paintwork and paths have been water blasted; as for the lawns, I've never seen them looking so good. Even the awful kikuyu has been dug out and replaced by new grass seed."

"Did you end up going to the police?"

"No... no I didn't. How could I? Truth is, I would have kept the person on as a house-guest! Thinking about it, I'm pretty sure it was a woman. One with excellent DIY skills, of course."

This surprises me. "Eh?"

"On the top of the vanity unit I found several black ring stains. In fact, I've just bought some Jiff from 'Woollies' to remove them."

"You've lost me, Mrs Peterson."

"Hair dye, Jane. I'm sure the rings were left from a woman's bottle of black hair dye."

My despair at never seeing Bailey again is complete. Not only is he probably using another false name, right now he could be walking around with totally different hair colouring. We could pass each other in Queen Street and I might not even recognise him.

Then I think of his eyes. The way they can crinkle up in sudden amusement or fill abruptly with shocking grief. I would know those eyes anywhere...

This evening, I half-heartedly start to work on the last chapter of *Atonement*. I spread out Bailey's crudely drawn storyboards, but it's hard to stay focused and the story doesn't flow or feel complete. In the end, I put them aside. There no longer seems any point in finishing it.

Two weeks later Mad is about to go on stage. I'm waiting in the wings trying to give moral support. Though to be honest, I'm probably more anxious than she is. She has to sing a solo, and the thing is, I don't even know if she can sing! Plus, the entire school is watching, along with everyone's parents, grandparents, younger siblings, friends and friends of friends; I swear I've never seen the school hall so packed. This could end up a totally mortifying, cringe-worthy spectacle.

"Break a leg," I whisper.

She flashes me a nervous grin.

I sneak back to the audience and sit down next to Mum. As Mad walks onto the stage, I glance across at Mum — she looks so proud. Oh God... I hope she's still wearing that look in a few minute's time.

Mad is dressed in skinny black trousers and a black hoodie — all the cast are dressed in casual contemporary gear but none quite as minimalistic or striking as my sister. The lights dim apart from one spotlight which now hovers over Mad. Her naturally hollow cheekbones and theatrical eye makeup give her a haunted look: a perfect Mary Magdalene. (Or is she just a terrified rabbit caught in the glare of headlights?) My hands are sweating; I've crossed all available fingers and toes. A hush descends over the audience with the only sound being the ring of someone's cell phone immediately behind me. I turn round and glare at the teenage offender. The girl quickly turns it off.

As Mad opens her mouth, I suck in my breath. Then she starts to sing *By My Side* and I am instantly mesmerised. As she slowly builds to a crescendo, her every note incredibly clear and pure, I think to myself: *My sister is AMAZING!* I look back at Mum. She has tears running down her cheeks, so I reach across and squeeze her hand. She grasps mine in return and repeats in a choked-up voice, "I didn't know, I didn't know."

I had no idea Mad could sing either, let alone stand on a big stage and confidently deliver a song like this. There is a distinctive quality to her voice, a subtle huskiness which I absolutely love, and she somehow manages to convey so much emotion and longing. I just wish Bailey was here to witness this. He believed in her all along.

Halfway through Mad's performance, I look back to check out the rest of the audience. They look equally spellbound and some of Mad's peers are just plain gobsmacked. For a second I swear I catch a glimpse of a tall trench-coated figure hovering behind the sea of heads. But when I stand up to get a better look, all I can see is the school janitor in his long overalls. The girl sitting behind hisses at me to sit down. Payback for my earlier glare. I plop back onto my seat, feeling irrationally disappointed and a bit of an idiot. Bailey is long gone...

Meanwhile, Mad has finished singing, and some poor pimply youth is having to follow in her shadow and spout his lines. I manage to catch Mad's eye and give her two thumbs up. She immediately winks at me. I sit back for the rest of the show and continue to bask in the reflected glory. Which is weird because a part of me always use to resent Mad's achievements rather than rejoice in them. Guess that shows just how much our relationship has changed.

007

At school in the New Year I keep my promise to Mum and start putting more effort into some of my other subjects, including maths. Being realistic, I will probably never get Excellences but I do get more Merits than Achieves nowadays. It seems a small price to pay, now that I've taken up art and graphic design. In those two subjects, I always get top marks.

Mad still looks skinny and I suspect it will be a long while before she'll be able to look at food without counting calories. But her periods have finally come back and she sings in the shower all the time. Next year she hopes to get into drama school to study musical theatre.

Mum is still dating 007. Actually, his name is Anthony Remmus and she's been seeing him for over two months. Today he is coming to our house for dinner and Mad and I will finally get to meet him properly. Until now it's just been polite doorway talk: *Hello Tony! I'm fine, thanks. Yes, it is nice weather today. I'll just get Mum for you.*

"I still think he's a bit old," I whisper to Mad when we are finally alone. We are in the kitchen making coffee after dinner, while Mum and Tony retire to the lounge.

"Shh! He might hear you. He's forty-six and, for the record, I think he's a hunk. Besides, the grey hair makes him look distinguished in a George Clooney sort of way."

"I guess. Have you noticed how they can't take their eyes off each other?"

"Yeah," she says. "I think it's really sweet. Apparently, Mum is the first woman he's dated since his wife died suddenly three years ago. His colleagues at work signed him up for the dating website without his knowledge. According to Mum, he was ropable when he found out. Then he saw Mum's photo, read her profile and the rest, as they say, is history."

"So how did she die?"

"Who?"

"His wife, silly."

"No idea. Not exactly light meal table conversation, is it? Besides, I don't think even Mum knows. Here, J.D., grab the sugar in case he wants some."

Mad calls me J.D. now. It's funny, but Bailey's legacy

surrounds us all in so many ways. I know he didn't exactly approve of our interference in Mum's love-life, but Mum wouldn't have dreamt of even going there if Bailey hadn't cut her hair and encouraged her to apply for the library job. As for Mad, I wonder if she would even be alive now if he hadn't picked up on her anorexia. And I wouldn't be pursuing a career as an artist — that's for sure.

I look across at Tony Remmus. He is sitting on our old threadbare couch with his arm casually draped around Mum's shoulder. There is something about him I really like. He feels solid and dependable — nothing 'arty-farty' about this guy. I try to imagine him as a father figure. It suddenly occurs to me that Mum is still young enough to have another child... I choke on the after-dinner mint I'm eating.

"So, tell me, Jane. What do you envisage doing after you leave school?"

I cough, frantically trying to dislodge a disconcerting image of a little George Clooney running round in nappies.

I realise Tony is still waiting for a reply. I decide now is as good a time as any to drop my bombshell. I clear my throat and say, "I'd like to be an illustrator of graphic novels and children's books."

There is a moment's silence and out of the corner of my eye I see Mad roll her eyes. We are both waiting for the fireworks.

Then Tony says, "Well, I'm not surprised. According to your mother, you have amazing talent in that area." Mum reaches out and squeezes his hand and they both smile across at me.

My mouth falls open. This is not the reaction I was expecting from my mother. Clearly, being in love involves a personality transplant.

Then Tony adds, "I have an eighteen-year-old son. If things had been different, I think you two would have really liked each other."

I hate the notion. I don't want Bailey replaced by some pimply wannabe.

Mad asks, "Where is your son now?"

Tony stiffens and replies, "Unfortunately, I have no idea. We are... estranged." Then he gruffly changes the subject.

After he leaves, I look up *estranged* on Google. I mean, seriously, who uses that word in conversation nowadays? It says: *alienated, separated, divided, apart, not speaking, at odds, on bad terms, disaffected...* So which is it? Or perhaps it's all of the above?

Mum and 007 are full-on throughout the rest of the summer and into autumn. Sometimes he arrives bearing gifts: flowers for Mum, tickets to the latest musical for Mad, a new drawing block and paints for moi, when I turned fifteen last month. It's so sweet of him. We all find him comfortable to be around. Dependable — not like my dad.

At Easter Tony suggests we go away together for a long 'family' weekend. An innocent and perfectly reasonable suggestion. Not some offer of a full-on weekend of sex for two. Mad is quite keen. So am I, for that matter. An all-expenses-paid weekend away — what's not to like? Surprisingly, it's Mum that goes into a total spin over the whole idea. It brings everything to a head.

"I don't know how to be intimate with Tony," she confides to Mad and me.

"You mean sex?" asks Mad awkwardly.

Mum goes a distinct shade of red. "No. The sex is just fine, thank you very much! It's just... he never talks about the past. Ever. It hangs over us like a black cloud. I can ask a perfectly natural question and he abruptly changes the subject. Or some innocent random comment can trigger a total shutdown. I'm starting to think it was a real mistake getting this involved."

I am still getting my head around the fact that Mum and Tony had been doing IT. Where exactly has IT been taking place? He never stays overnight, so perhaps they do it at his place. Oh God, surely it wasn't happening in his car...

Thankfully, Mad interrupts my runaway freight train of disturbing erotic imagery. "I thought you two got on just fine? You guys are always chatting."

"Yes, we talk about *things* but never about feelings. Tony is the strong, silent type. Believe me; I've tried everything to get him to open up. I feel as though I could have really loved this man if he would just let his guard down. It's like a part of him wants to move on, but he's haunted by the past. To be honest — I can't handle living in the wake of his emotional vacuum any longer."

"What about Easter?" I ask.

Mum sighs, tosses back her hair and seems to make a decision. "Easter is off," she declares, followed by: "I'm going to end things between us before either of us gets really hurt."

I note her face has gone all pale and pinched.
Uh-oh. Me thinks you are already too late...

Later that evening Mum does end it. Just like that. I confess I hover behind the closed lounge door and try to listen in. At least she has the decency to do it in person, but she's not exactly giving him an explanation. She's just employing the broken record technique, repeating, "I'm sorry, Tony, it's over."

I catch a brief glimpse of Tony's face in the doorway afterwards. He looks like a stunned mullet and I swear his body has shrunk. Poor bugger.

For several days he tries phoning to change her mind. Mum is always friendly but firm, and plays that same record, "I'm sorry, it's over." And she wears that set *look*. I know from personal experience it's useless to argue with The Look, but it takes a while to register with Tony.

Mum stops answering the phone, so he tries emailing; she changes her email address. He writes letters; she scrawls RETURN TO SENDER on the envelopes. He even sends handmade chocolates from Devonport. Mum returns those too (but only after I managed to sneak a couple of the divine coffee creams for Mad and me). Then a spectacular bouquet of red roses arrives by courier — perfect blooms only partially opened; they will continue to live for many days, despite having their stalks abruptly severed. For a moment Mum does hesitate. I watch as her fingers trace the message on the small attached card. Then her face hardens, she carefully removes the card, and asks Mad to drop the flowers off at the local rest

home where she used to work. I'm pretty sure Mum never even acknowledges their receipt.

He finally gets the message after that.

No more 007.

I feel irrationally disappointed. Over these last few weeks I have got used to Tony's comfortable presence in all our lives. Looking back, I think what got me was the lack of early warning signs. There was no one major nuclear argument between them. No harsh words fired off like well-aimed missiles. Not even the light artillery of constant bickering. Nope — I never saw it coming. The end of their relationship crept up on us all like a lethal odourless gas.

Now I hear her sobbing into a pillow late at night and immediately feel guilty. As autumn slips inevitably into winter, depressing grey skies and relentless rain perfectly reflect Mum's mood. Bailey had told me it would all end up pear-shaped.

Lord of the Manor

In early August our landlord, Mr R.J. Baverstock, comes round. That's how he always signs his emails: R.J. Baverstock. Even Mum doesn't know what his first name is and he's been our landlord for over seven years; that's half of my entire life. Mad says it's probably something boring and old-fashioned like Reginald Jeffrey. Personally, I think it stands for Repulsive Jerk. Sounds harsh, but seriously — you only have to look at the guy!

Right now his large beer belly is entering the kitchen ahead of the rest of his ample body and he plonks himself down on a chair at our rimu table, spreads out his tree-trunk legs and leans back like Lord of the Manor. Technically, I suppose he is.

After all, he does own the roof over our heads and every single wall around us.

He's wearing a pale pink shirt that has the unfortunate effect of emphasizing his florid complexion. His red veins stand out like a map of London's underground and I watch his eyes follow Mad while Mum makes a pot of tea. That surprises me. Why is she even making him a cup of tea? Usually she avoids talking to the guy and any communication is via email or text.

I notice his eyes are bloodshot and they quickly settle on Mad's breasts. Mum also notices. She plonks his tea down unceremoniously and it splashes up at his shirt. *Oops.*

He glares and furiously starts dabbing at the silk material. "I'm an extremely busy and important man, Mrs Dawson," he barks. "But I'm a decent sort," *Yeah, right...* "And I've personally come round to give you ninety days' notice. I want you and your family out of here even sooner if possible. The house is going on the market and—"

"Mr Baverstock, I'm fully aware you intend to sell and I'd like to make you a private offer on this house," interrupts Mum.

"Eh? You what?"

"I want to make you a private offer," repeats Mum.

I glance across at Mad. She looks as bemused as I feel.

Mr Baverstock leans even further back in his chair until the slender wooden spindles start to creak. Then he begins to laugh. It's not a pleasant sound and I notice his beer gut is bouncing up and down like pink blancmange.

I really wish I was Proton and could blast him off the planet. At the very least, I hope Mum will make some scathing comment or give him The Look. Surprisingly, she doesn't.

Instead she smiles and then produces a document from the drawer of the old kitchen table, saying, "I had my solicitor draw up a sales and purchase agreement. I believe my offer to be fair and reasonable, taking into account it is a cash, unconditional offer and you will be saving a considerable amount on the absence of estate agent fees."

Mr Baverstock's jaw sags. He closes his legs and leans over the document, flattening his stomach against the table. He pulls a pair of glasses out of a top pocket and peers through them. Then he splutters, "Naturally my own solicitor will need to check this over."

"Naturally," says Mum.

He stands up and adds brusquely, "I'll be in touch." He hasn't touched his cup of tea.

After he leaves, Mad and I just stare at Mum open-mouthed. She gives a girlish giggle and says, "Did I forget to mention the proceeds of your father's estate have finally come through?"

Six weeks later Mum is officially Lady of the Manor, Mad and I are the proud owners of our very own laptops and our old car is replaced by one that actually starts when the key is turned. We all go out to dinner to celebrate at a flash restaurant in the City called Four Steps to Heaven. (Up until now 'dining out' had meant eating fish and chips at our local takeaway).

We climb four wide concrete steps to enter the restaurant and are led by a penguin-clad waiter to a candlelit table. Mum and I chose the schnitzel stuffed with ham and camembert and I swear it just seems to melt in our mouths. Mad actually chooses a huge steak, medium rare and bathed in field mushrooms. She eats every mouthful. We all demolish the garlic bread, dripping with lashings of pungent butter and devour the generous servings of tiramisu dessert.

It feels so good to watch Mad eating like a healthy teen again and to see Mum's eyes lit up with the excitement of it all, pushing Tony from her mind, at least for these couple of hours.

But afterwards, as I lay back home in bed with my flying helmet fastened like a security blanket around my head, I realise I would have traded that incredible gourmet meal for soggy cucumber sandwiches on a windswept Waiheke beach, if it had meant I could have shared them again with Bailey.

Palindromes

It's the second week of September and my English teacher, Mrs Watts, has come down with the flu. Actually, half the class is off sick and there are all these warnings in the school toilets to wash hands thoroughly. It's a strain of swine flu that is spreading across Auckland.

We have a new relieving teacher, Carla Jennings, who is telling us all about palindromes. She's young and enthusiastic; it's infectious and I'm actually enjoying today's class. A palindrome is a word or sentence that reads the same forward as it does backward. She reads out a famous example by some guy called Leigh Mercer: "A man, a plan, a canal – Panama!" It's very clever and I just know Bailey would have loved it. He was always playing around with words.

Then Miss Jennings gets us to write out our names backwards to see if any of us has a palindrome. Anna Taylor and Hannah McKenzie both have first names that read the same each way. Mark Jamieson is sitting alongside me and glances across at my surname spelt backwards and whispers, "How's it going Noswad." I give him a withering look that even Proton would have been proud of.

I start writing down all our family names but there isn't even one palindrome. So on a whim I write 'Bailey' and get 'Yeliab' which is almost as bad as Noswad. Then I reverse 'Summer' and it spells 'Remmus'. Afterwards, I just sit there staring at the sheet of paper. I even write the letters down again, slower this time, in case I have made a mistake. I haven't. It's definitely Remmus; the exact same surname as Mum's 007.

"What's up?" asks Mad at lunchtime.

I am still clutching the same piece of paper, trying to decide at what point coincidence becomes more than that and transforms into fate. I can't make up my mind. It's a relief to hand over my dilemma to Mad.

"Oh my God!" she exclaims in a shocked tone.

"Do you think it's a coincidence?" I ask.

"No way. Tony Remmus must be Bailey's father!"

"You think? Tony said his estranged son was eighteen. Bailey was only fifteen."

"Bailey lied about his name and his parents. What makes you suddenly think he was telling the truth about his age? Always did think the guy looked mature for his age."

"So what should I do?"

"It's not just *your* problem, J.D. Mum's never been the same since that breakup with Tony. We'll figure out a solution together."

This is one of those times when it feels really good to have an older sister on my side. I realise it's a feeling that has become increasingly familiar since Bailey entered our lives a year earlier.

After much deliberation, our solution is for me to suddenly come down with the flu. I wake up the next morning complaining of aches and pains, a headache and a blocked nose. I am careful not to overdo things: I don't want Mum staying home or taking me to the doctor. Mad reassures her that all I need is bed rest and paracetamol. I do feel guilty when Mum produces a special tonic for me, using freshly squeezed lemons, honey and glycerine. I draw the line at the Vicks ointment she also wants to rub onto my chest.

"That's okay, Mum. I can do that," I mumble awkwardly.

Mad has already loaded extra funds onto my Hop card last night, to cover bus fares into the City and back. Tony Remmus is a detective assigned to the Auckland Central Police Station and yesterday evening Mad left a message on his answerphone saying she was Laura Dawson. Actually, she sounds just like Mum and people often get them mixed up over the phone.

She said, "Could you please meet me at midday outside the

University Wedding Cake. There is something very important I wish to discuss."

"Are you sure he'll know which building it is?" I asked Mad afterwards.

"Yeah, course he will. Everyone knows that building."

I had wanted her to say 'high noon' but Mad thought it was too melodramatic. Personally, I thought that was quite appropriate in the circumstances. After all, I am about to tell him that his estranged son had enjoyed Mum's Sunday roast through the whole of last spring.

The Wedding Cake

The Auckland University Clock Tower, formerly the Old Arts Building, was designed by an American dude in the 1920s. He was apparently inspired by the Art Nouveaux movement and, despite being American, he did think to include some nice touches: carvings of New Zealand birds like the kaka and kea, native ponga fronds and even seed pods from flax bushes.

I remember all this useless information because when I was ten, Mum brought Mad and me one evening to see the huge Christmas tree that stands each December in the building's foyer. (We couldn't afford our own tree that year, so I guess it was her way of compensating). Anyway, the vividly white, highly ornate and organic Clock Tower, inevitably nicknamed the Wedding Cake, stands out like a sore thumb on a modern university campus composed primarily of boring Lego-shaped blocks.

Tony Remmus also stands out like a sore thumb among the dozens of t-shirted university students milling around the tower. For starters, he is dressed in a suit. It's light grey and he's wearing a black shirt, complete with grey tie, to match the suit. Even the picnic hamper in his right hand looks incredibly out of place — he probably picked it up from Smith and Caughey's fine produce department.

He is early but I was earlier and now I'm standing behind a tree across the road trying to pluck up the courage to approach him. As usual, I'm hiding under my aviator hat. Pathetic, I know. I look across at him and realise I had totally forgotten how determined the set of his jaw line can be. If he was a detective investigating a case for me, I would feel reassured. As a criminal, I would feel decidedly uneasy. Considering Mad had impersonated Mum, I'd lied about my illness, and we'd deceived them both, right now I am definitely feeling more like the latter.

Mad and I had agreed that I had to be the one with the imaginary flu and come to this meeting. (Mum still worries about the long term effects of Mad's anorexia and would have stayed home if Mad had said she was sick). Now I wish I hadn't agreed so readily. The clock chimes midday and I take a deep breath, ignoring the thumping in my chest and uncomfortable, sweaty palms. I immerge from behind the tree and he spots me immediately. He strides across the narrow road before I even have a chance to step on the black and white crossing.

"Jane! I wasn't ex— Laura, is she okay?" Fear quickly overtakes the surprise in his voice. I realise I have caught him off-guard. He obviously thinks something has happened to Mum, and now I feel like a total shit.

"Mum's fine," I say quickly. "She's at work and doesn't know anything about this meeting."

"Her phone message—"

"That was Madeleine. They sound very alike. I'm sorry. It seemed like a good idea at the time..."

Tony inclines his head and gives me a rueful grin. "Looks like I've been set up." Then he adds, "I hope you're hungry and like smoked chicken."

I assure him I love smoked chicken and follow him over to a quiet shady spot in Albert Park, underneath a massive ombu tree. As kids Mad and I used to play in the bizarre roots and hollow cavities of this particular tree, pretending to hunt mythical beasts and giggling over the blurred messages carved into the bark — sometimes we'd even find the discarded bedding of a homeless person or perhaps it was left by lovers.

Tony takes off his jacket, removes his tie, rolls up his shirt sleeves and suddenly he doesn't look so out of place anymore. As we start to eat, I have to admit, somewhat grudgingly, that he looks rather attractive for an older guy. I can see why Mum chose him as her lover... I also realise I am surprisingly hungry and eagerly tuck into the chicken and French bread.

At one point I look up. He has cut his hair since I last saw him — a real short buzz cut — and now I notice, just above his left eyebrow, a small irregular pockmark. I suck in my breath: the mark of Kane!

"Jane. You're staring at me. Have I got a glob of mayonnaise on my nose or something?"

I swallow nervously and shake my head.

"Here, eat," he adds softly. "Then we can talk and you can tell me what this is all about."

I put aside my misgivings — I am *very* hungry — and together we make a surprising dent in the huge mountain of food. Turns out he packed it all himself, even adding cherry tomatoes. So much for my giving the credit to Smith and Caughey's. I make a mental note not to keep leaping to false conclusions.

"More?" he asks afterwards.

I groan and reply, "As a well brought up child I should probably say, 'no thank you, I've had sufficient'. But as a teenager, I shall simply say, I'm stuffed!"

He throws back his head and laughs, and in that moment it's like I am talking to Bailey. How could I ever have missed that resemblance? I wonder if Bailey's true hair colouring is the same light brown as Tony's used to be... I can still make out traces of brown in between the grey that now dominates his closely cropped buzz.

"Ready to talk, Jane?"

"I guess. You've been really good about all this."

"I figured you did it for a good reason."

"Yeah." For a moment I fiddle with the leather straps on my

flying hat. To be honest, I'm not exactly sure where to start. And now there is the added complication of the mark of Kane... would Bailey approve of this meeting or would he be appalled?

I take a deep breath and, for better or worse, I launch straight in: "A year ago a teenage boy called Bailey Summer walked into our lives. He lived in our street, attended my school, mowed our lawns and shared our Sunday roast. He wrote stories and I illustrated them. He became my soul mate."

Tony gives me a bemused look. "I think your mother may have mentioned him. Sounds like a nice kid. But I don't get what this has to do with—"

I cut him off. "Mr Remmus, I think that boy was your son."

Tony runs trembling fingers through his short hair and says softly, "Please, call me Tony. And whatever gave you that idea?"

"Palindromes."

"What?"

"A palindrome is—"

"I know what a palindrome is."

"Well, strictly speaking it's not a palindrome anyway, it's a semordnilap, which makes a completely different word when spelt in reverse."

"Your point is?" Now he sounds irritated.

I opt for the direct approach. "Summer is Remmus spelt backwards. And the boy's upper body was covered in horrific burn scars."

The blood seems to literally drain from Tony Remmus's face. I suddenly feel nervous again.

He mutters, "Dear God — *I don't believe it...* I've spent

months combing the whole of New Zealand and all along he was right here in Auckland!" He jerks his head up and I'm shocked by the pain I can see in those brown eyes of his, so like his son's.

"Jane, tell me, where is he now?" His voice sounds urgent and raw with emotion.

I shrug. "He never told me where he was going. He left the Pakuranga area at the beginning of last December. But if I did know, I probably wouldn't tell you anyway. He was my friend and he was running away from you. My loyalty lies with him."

Tony gives a soft grunt and I think he's pissed off with me. But then he says, "Adam is lucky to have such a loyal friend."

Now it's my turn to be surprised. "Is that his name? Adam?"

"Uh-huh. Named after his mother's father."

In a funny sort of way, Bailey had tried to tell me his real name: *J.D., I'd like you to meet my father, Adam...* Then I wonder why he had chosen the name Bailey. An image of our small kitchen springs to mind. On our sideboard sits a bottle of Bailey's Irish Cream given to Mum as a thank you by the rest-home residents. Mum's a teetotaller so it sits permanently unopened. That time Bailey stood there in his trenchcoat and first introduced himself, the bottle of liqueur would have sat in full view.

"I think he named himself after a liqueur!" I blurt out.

"Excuse me?"

I sigh, "Forget it. So, are you going to tell me what happened between you guys, or are you going to do the strong silent routine and shut me out, just like you did with my mum?"

"Christ. Talk about hitting a man when he's down. Is that why Laura broke it off with me? She never really explained. She just kept repeating 'it's over' like a broken record."

I'm aware I'm entering dangerous territory here. I tread carefully with my words.

"Mum felt your past was preventing you from living fully in the present with her."

He gives another soft grunt.

I think I've just hit the same brick wall Mum ran into.

It's solid.

"Look. I'm sorry if I've upset you, Tony. I guess I just wanted confirmation that the boy I knew was really your son. He's lost to us both now. You've probably got heaps of work to get back to. Thanks for lunch and all that. I'll leave you to it." I go to stand.

Tony is even quicker and leaps up, effectively blocking my path. He tilts his head and gives a self-deprecating smile. It's tinged with sadness.

"Jane, stay. Please... I'm not good at expressing my feelings and I have developed an unfortunate habit of running away from vulnerability at a hundred miles an hour, especially if it's my own. But bear with me and I will try to tell you our story, Adam's and mine. And... the story of how my wife and young daughter died."

I gasp and abruptly sit back down again, saying, "I didn't know you had also lost a daughter."

"Yes." He sucks in his breath, as if poised on the edge of a precipice. When he releases it again he whispers hoarsely, "Her name was Holly — a Christmas baby. She was my... joy."

The fragility of his tone reminds me of the coloured glass baubles I'd once seen years ago swinging on the very tips of delicate pine needles on the 'Wedding Cake' Christmas tree.

Tony looks across at me then and says, "In fact, Jane, you remind me of her a little. She was only eleven when she died but you have the same vivid blue eyes."

"Was Bai— Adam close to his sister?"

"Very. There was a four year age difference but they used to spend summer holidays together at their grandparents. Holly worshipped him. To her, he was like a superhero. When Adam and I had our major fallout she took it really badly."

"Why did you fall out?"

Tony stiffens. It's hard to read him because he has deliberately averted his eyes. Then he seems to make a decision and looks straight at me. His eyes are filled with guilt and remorse. They look suspiciously watery.

"On Adam's fifteenth birthday, he announced he was gay. I—", Tony swallows awkwardly. "I confess I handled it badly. I didn't exactly order him out of the house, but we were barely on speaking terms for days afterwards. To be honest — I made some unforgivable comments. How I reacted is something I shall always regret. If I could have that time replayed again, I would have acknowledged his courage and honesty and told him I was proud to be his father."

"How did his mum react?"

"Elizabeth? She took it all in her stride. I think she had suspected as much all along. I guess that bond between mother and son is so strong that it can operate at a non-verbal level. Lizzie and Holly tried to act as a buffer between Adam and me."

I lay back and digest this new information. None of what I have just heard surprises me. It explains why Bailey had felt drawn to me at our first meeting in that shopping mall. Apparently I have his sister's eyes and there is even the same age difference between us. And he had openly told Mad he was gay right from the start. He had been warier with me, though. Perhaps my reaction was the one that counted and he was afraid of how I would respond...

I turn round, prop myself up on my elbow and ask, "Tony, have you ever acted in plays and stuff?"

"Me? Good God no — what a strange question. I'm far too reserved."

Okay, so clearly Bailey was indulging his warped sense of humour when he said his dad was an actor.

"Was Elizabeth a make-up artist?"

"Yes — yes, she was. But she originally trained as a hairdresser."

At least Bailey was telling the truth about his mum's occupation then.

"Adam loved to watch her," continues Tony. "I remember the time he borrowed her scissors — he must have only been about seven years old — and cut off all of Holly's ringlets. I was furious, but Lizzie just laughed and pointed out he'd done a very tidy, professional job. Holly was delighted because everyone said she now looked like a little girl and not a toddler."

"So how did they both die?"

Tony goes silent, and I mentally kick myself for being so blunt. For a moment I think I have pushed him too hard. He just sits there and rests his head in both his hands. Then he turns towards me. He suddenly looks much older, the lines of his face etched deeply with grief.

I know I am going to hear of events that had prompted Bailey, years later, to write about the appalling destruction of Proton's world.

I feel sick.

Gods and Monsters

Beneath Albert Park there is an elaborate network of tunnels built during World War II as air-raid shelters. The entrances were all sealed off after the War and then forgotten for decades. It becomes very clear to me that Tony Remmus may have sealed his past away in the dark tunnels of his mind, but, unlike the ones in the park beneath us, he has not forgotten one detail of their tortuous route.

"It happened three and a half years ago on the twenty-first of February. Some dates can never be forgotten, Jane. It was a Saturday. Adam insisted on taking part in the parade."

"Parade?"

"The Auckland Pride Parade for the LGBT community — years ago it used to be called the Hero Parade. Bailey had only recently 'come out' and he insisted on attending — at the time I thought he was rubbing my face in it. We were living in Drury. I refused to drive him, even though a large contingency of uniformed police were taking part that year, wanting to show their support. Actually, I think that was half the problem. Some were colleagues of mine... I guess I was embarrassed and, deep down, I felt ashamed that my own son was gay. So Lizzie announced she would take him. Of course, Holly insisted on going too."

I feel uneasy. "Tony, please. You don't need to do this. I realise this is painful for you..."

He sighs. "Actually, Jane, I really think I do. Your mother was right: I've kept the past locked away inside for far too long."

So I sit here in Albert Park and listen, oblivious to the comings and goings of the students around us. At one point I hear a grey warbler, the bird song emanating from the twisted branches of the ombu tree above. I even wonder if it is the same bird that had sung to Bailey and me that afternoon on Waiheke. A fanciful notion, I know. But a comforting one.

The sweet sound fades away into the background.

In my mind's eye I am left with a vivid image of thousands of spectators lining either side of Ponsonby Road — men, women and children all excitedly waiting to watch the sixty floats, led by Dykes on Bikes, noisily pass by. Each year the parade gets bigger, better and more colourfully outrageous. I've been a couple of times recently with Mum and Mad; a real blast. But not that year. The theme that particular year was Gods and Monsters. According to Tony, even our current prime minister took part as a Labour MP.

Tony was watching the parade on television in his living room at home. He combed the footage of the crowds, but couldn't spot Lizzie or Holly. He did, however, catch a fleeting glimpse of his son.

"Adam was dressed like a heroic Greek God. He was radiating happiness."

He falls silent, so I prompt him gently: "And?"

"After the parade, Liz rang me to say they were going to grab a pizza to eat before driving home. She sounded... so bubbly — on a high. I remember hearing Holly in the background, giggling. I regretted not going then. I wanted to share their joy. It was the last time I ever heard their voices."

He goes quiet. I'm aware the park has emptied; lunch-time is over and students are rapidly filling up the lecture theatres. In the distance I can hear the steady sounds of traffic coming from Wellesley Street. A car horn blares out and another one furiously responds in a fit of road rage. Way in the distance there is the piercing sound of an ambulance, no doubt weaving its way to Auckland Hospital along Symonds Street.

The traffic noise triggers a memory. I was only eleven at the time of that parade, but I still recall the horror — it was all over the news and images were spread, as if from a war-zone, across the front of the *Sunday Herald*. I didn't even want Mum to drive me to school the following Monday. I insisted on walking. By the end of the week, when it poured with rain, memory had sufficiently dulled and I finally agreed to enter what I now considered to be a metal coffin.

I say, tentatively, "There was a horrendous pile-up on the Southern Motorway, after that parade... I think a petrol tanker overturned."

I glance across at Tony's white face and realise I've hit the jackpot.

"Yes — they were caught in the middle of that carnage." He swallows, clearly struggling to gain control of his emotions. Finally he whispers, "It was later established that a campervan with a family of Swedish tourists pulled out directly in front of the petrol tanker. The tanker driver tried to take evasive action, but he clipped the campervan and then lost control of his own vehicle, ploughing across the median strip straight into the path of oncoming traffic. Meanwhile, the campervan spun round and hit Lizzie's Toyota, smashing into the driver's side at over 100 kilometres an hour."

"Oh my God..."

"According to the coroner's report, Liz and Holly died instantly from massive head and internal injuries. Adam was in the passenger seat and miraculously escaped with just whiplash and some minor cuts."

"But his burns?"

"He got those afterwards. I read his detailed police statement and poured over the graphic crash scene photos. I'll never forget one particular image: the driver's side of their red Toyota was peeled back like the lid of a sardine can; the contents a mangled mess. Like scrunched up tin foil. Unrecognizable."

Tony looks ill. I wait patiently for him to continue.

He draws in a deep breath, exhales and says, "He pulled his mum and little sister's lifeless bodies free of the wreckage. There was nothing he could do for them... he must have felt devastated... utterly helpless and horrified; he's never talked to me about it."

I think of that first chapter in *Atonement* where Proton loses his entire family; the vivid descriptions of what he saw and felt and heard; perhaps one day I'll let Tony read it.

I add gently, "What happened then?"

"In his report, Adam described hearing frantic cries coming from the campervan. He ran over and instantly saw the driver was dead, slumped against the steering wheel with his head partially severed. Alongside him a woman was hysterical, crying out in Swedish and she kept pointing behind her. Smoke from the engine was filling up the cab, making it hard for Adam to see. He peered through the blood-splattered glass and spotted two little fair-haired girls in the back, still strapped in their booster seats. They stared back at him, wide-eyed and both were quietly sobbing 'Mamma'; one word that seems to be universal in any language."

"Oh God, those poor little kids. What happened next?"

"The impact of the crash had concertinaed and jammed all the side doors, so in desperation, Adam kicked in a rear window. He somehow managed to reach in, unfasten the seatbelts of both children, and grab one child under each arm. Meanwhile, another bystander rescued the distraught mother.

Only moments later a gas bottle exploded inside the van. To say they were bloody lucky is an understatement. Witnesses at the scene said that afterwards, the little girls kept calling out to him: *superhjälte! superhjälte!*"

"Is that Swedish for superhero?"

Tony nods. "Adam was still wearing his Pride Parade costume. The twin girls were just three years old. It must have been the only thing about that appalling night which made any damn sense."

"So that's how he got burnt? With the gas bottle exploding?"

"Amazingly, no. Adam was still basically unharmed and had returned to the grass verge. He was bending over the bodies of Lizzie and Holly. I gather someone offered to cover their faces, but Adam became extremely agitated, pushing the person away, saying his mum and little sister wouldn't be able to breathe. Other cars had stopped and people were helping to carry the crash survivors as far away from the petrol tanker and burning campervan as possible. Fire and ambulance crews were still on their way."

"Were other vehicles involved?"

"There were three others, including a young motorcyclist who never stood a chance; a promising medical student who was thrown thirty metres by the impact. He's now a living vegetable. I still visit him — he's in a special care facility in Epsom. He has no real awareness — he looks right through you — which his parents find unnerving. But he does enjoy his food. He has to be spoon-fed, but he has a smile to die for if you pop a dark-chocolate ginger in his mouth. I suspect I visit more to remind myself that at least my own son is walking around somewhere, thinking and talking, even if I can't see and hear him."

I'm busy thinking about all the people the police would have had to contact after that terrible night. Including Tony. I mutter out loud, "Five devastated families..."

"It was almost six: after the gas bottle exploded, no one dared approach the tanker to help rescue the driver; it would have been suicide. I honestly don't know if that registered with Adam."

"He must have been overwhelmed by grief."

Tony gives another nod. Then he adds, "I'm not sure I could have done what he did next."

"What do you mean?"

"Eyewitnesses say he stood up, having finally covered Lizzie and Holly's faces himself, and just stared at the tanker. Then he suddenly sprinted across to the upturned cab, wrenched open the door, and struggled to free the unconscious driver. Adam was a slender fifteen-year-old and the driver was no light-weight. He was dragging the guy backwards into a ditch, they were almost clear, when a trail of petrol from the tanker inevitably reached the burning campervan. People reported hearing the explosion from as far away as Ardmore. Pictures even fell off walls in nearby houses."

"*Jeez* — it's a miracle either of them ever survived!"

"Yeah... the tanker driver regained consciousness just in time to witness the massive fireball roll over the top of his head. He escaped with singed eyebrows. He also had concussion and fractured ribs, but they were caused by the collision, not the explosion."

Tony took a deep breath and then continued, his voice ragged, "It was Adam's chest and arms that bore the brunt. Full-thickness burns that turned his skin black, right through to the subcutaneous tissue. Thankfully, my son's head was bent down, which protected his actual face, although his long hair was completely burnt off. The driver later told a reporter it was like Armageddon and he thought he'd gone to hell. He'd 'come to' and seen a screaming apparition, hair on fire, towering over him like a monster... it was only later that he found out the truth. He swore then that Adam was a hero."

I shudder at the thought of Bailey being in so much pain.

"He *was* a hero!"

"Yes. Yes, he was. And it was all *my* fault," whispered Tony hoarsely. "If I had just accepted Adam and offered him the support he needed, we would never have argued that day. I would have been driving the car, and perhaps I could have avoided the collision..."

I feel sick inside. Even after all these years, Tony was still playing the 'what if' game. Meanwhile, I'm replaying the image of a desperate Bailey pulling his mum and sister clear of the wreckage, only to find they were both dead; his own finger now on a self-destruct button.

Eventually I say, "What happened after that?"

"I was in shock," says Tony. "I was a volatile brew of grief and despair. I remember I felt a desperate need to attach blame. Adam was recovering in the burns unit at Auckland Hospital.

I went in to see him."

I have a feeling I know where this is heading. "I guess you'd kinda like to replay that conversation differently too?"

Tony gives a painful grimace. "I totally screwed up. At one point I lost control and yelled at him. I told him it was all *his* fault his mother and kid sister had died. I said they were only travelling on the motorway that night because of his bloody gay parade. I even stated I would never forgive him and nothing he could do would ever atone for that. It was a monstrous thing to say. Not a day goes by when I don't think about that conversation and feel intense regret."

"Shit... that certainly explains a lot." I was thinking of the name of our graphic novel, *Atonement* and Bailey's reaction after he cut my hair and I told him all was forgiven. But all I say is, "What happened then?"

"After Adam was discharged from hospital he chose to live with his grandparents and complete his schooling on Waiheke Island. But the death of their only daughter and young granddaughter really affected them. Adam's grandad died shortly afterwards, following a series of strokes and Doris, Adam's grandma, contracted double pneumonia three months later and had to go into hospital. She never came out. The last time I saw Adam was at his grandmother's funeral. He had just turned sixteen. He left school and the island immediately afterwards and I've been searching for him ever since."

"Oh my God... So in the space of a year, both your worlds totally disintegrated. No wonder Bailey, I mean Adam, took off! And it's not surprising you shut down emotionally; losing both a wife and a child would be almost too much to bear."

Tony is silent for a moment, and then he states, "Now it's like I have lost both my children. Jane, all I want to do is find my son and tell him how deeply sorry I am." His voice is choked full with emotion as he adds, "I want to tell him I'm proud of him and there is nothing to forgive. He is a real hero in my eyes; he saved so many lives that day and now I honestly don't give a damn what his sexuality is. He can be a gay cross-dressing transvestite and I'd still accept him. He's my son and I love him, that's all that matters."

I tentatively reach out my right hand and he grasps it blindly. He is sobbing and the resemblance between father and son is now uncanny. He looks just like Bailey did that last time I saw him on the Howick bus.

A few minutes later he removes his hand from mine and blows his nose loudly on a big white handkerchief.

I choose my words carefully and say, "You Remmus guys are obviously as bad as each other."

Tony raises a surprised eyebrow.

I add, "What happened that terrible evening was an appalling and tragic accident. You both need to stop beating yourselves up over it. Your wife and daughter died instantly and never suffered. You two guys have never stopped suffering. I reckon Elizabeth and Holly would be horrified if they knew how hard you are on yourselves. They'd want you to reconcile, move forwards and find some joy in life again. And for the record, I'm pretty sure your son is just gay, not a cross-dresser."

Tony gives a shaky laugh. "You are very wise for a fifteen-year-old, Jane. But I will need to *find* Adam first. I've combed both the North and South Islands. He hasn't applied for a passport to leave the country — I've checked of course. He's got to be hiding somewhere... someone must have seen him."

"Who has seen the nest of the kuaka?"

"I beg your pardon?"

"It's an old Maori riddle. Trying to find your son in New Zealand is like looking for a kuaka or godwit's nest. Mmm... so tell me, what happened to the Waiheke bach that belonged to Elizabeth's parents?"

"It's still there. I never had the heart to sell it. It's even got things from Holly's childhood... She and Adam used to spend their summer holidays there. Deep down I'd hoped Adam would reappear. I was going to offer it to him, rent-free, so he could pursue his passion as a writer. He always loved the island."

"Did Holly have a dolls' house, with crooked windows and crooked steps?"

"Yes! Her grandad made it for her one Christmas. How could you possibly know that?"

I shrug and ask, "So when was the last time you checked out the old bach?"

"Months ago. In fact, not since Easter. I was going to suggest we all go there to stay for the long Easter weekend, before your mum ended our relationship. You don't really think Adam would pick somewhere so obvious, surely?"

"I think, Tony, your son is very astute. He would assume you would take that attitude. Who else but a detective would overlook their own back yard. Besides, he's like a godwit —

drawn back to the same familiar place."

Tony frowns. "You've just lost me again. Besides, no electricity has been used — I would have immediately noticed any difference in the monthly bill."

"He could have used candles for lighting. And isn't there a wood stove?"

"Indeed, there is."

"So maybe he used that to heat the place over the winter months. And to cook on. He's smart and would know you would check the bill."

Tony looks pensive. He rubs the small pockmark above his left brow. Then he slowly turns to me and exclaims, "Christ! I do believe you could be right." Then he suddenly frowns and says, "But how the devil should I approach Adam, without scaring him off again?"

My brain starts to work overtime — I can feel a definite plan forming.

Long Lost Son of the Lord Protector

"If this is your idea of a joke, Madeleine, it's in extremely bad taste."

Mum sounds furious and I mean at 'gritting teeth' stage. I am secretly relieved that Mad had volunteered to tell her about the phone impersonation and today's events at Albert Park.

"It's no joke, Mum. Jane twigged that Bailey Summer was really Tony Remmus's son, Adam. She confronted Tony over a picnic lunch."

At this point I decide to add, "He told me all about the accident that killed his wife and daughter. He even broke down and cried."

"Nonsense! Now I know you are both making this up. A joke that is not only in bad taste, but it's also downright cruel. The Tony I knew would never let his guard down, let alone in the middle of a public park. And to my knowledge, he never even had a dau—

I interrupt, "Her name was Holly. And this is no bad joke, Mum. It's been three and a half years since their deaths. Tony desperately wants to reconcile with his son. There's something else you should know — Bai — I mean Adam, is gay. That's why they fell out."

Mum raises an amused eyebrow. "Of course Bailey's gay, dear. Do you honestly think I'd have left a gorgeous young man, who looked like a cross between Poldark and Adam Lambert, alone with either of my two teenage daughters if he wasn't?"

Now it's my turn to be surprised. Seems like I was the last to find out in our family. I obviously have a faulty gaydar. I add, "And Tony wants you to give him another chance."

Her face softens. "Did he actually say that?"

"His exact words were: *Tell your mum that while the old Tony would have run away from deep emotions at a hundred miles an hour; the new Tony will wade in with his gumboots on'.*"

"Good Lord!" Then she goes silent and focuses on some imaginary point above our heads. After what feels like an eternity, she appears to make up her mind about something. I hold my breath.

She looks directly at us and says, "No doubt you two herberts have a plan. So what *exactly* is it?"

I breathe out in relief and give Mad a grin. With Mum on board, now we really stand a fighting chance.

Tony rings Mum this evening on our landline and they seem to be on the phone for ages. Finally she puts the receiver down and now her face is flushed, but all she says is, "Tony's just booked his car on the vehicular ferry. It leaves for Waiheke from Half Moon Bay on Saturday morning. He'll pick us all up from here, so we'll need to be ready early."

"What about food?" I ask. I want every detail to be perfect.

"Tony said he would bring a coolie bin of sausages and a couple of bottles of tomato sauce. I told him we'd bring plenty of fresh bread and onions."

"What about a camping stove to cook the hotdogs on?"

"Not necessary. Apparently the Waiheke Council provide barbeques at all the main beaches and they even supply the firewood."

"Sweet," I reply.

So now all I have to do is finish Bailey's and my graphic novel. It wouldn't be such a big deal except today is Wednesday and I need to get it in tomorrow's mail by five o'clock. Hopefully it will then be delivered by Saturday morning. It has to arrive on Waiheke before we all do.

I dig out the storyboards Bailey had given me on the bus. I'd never liked his last chapter. Proton had taken off into the sunset and left everything unresolved. Now I'm going to completely rewrite it. I sharpen my pencils and set to work. Mum has cleared a place for me at the kitchen table and she and Mad are taking turns to bring me hot Milo drinks. At midnight Mum insists I go to bed.

At school the next day I spend the whole of my lunch hour frantically drawing, and after school I dash home to go over the finishing touches. Mad hovers anxiously in the doorway. At 4.30 p.m. I finally declare it finished and hand the completed manuscript over to Mad. She immediately places it in a padded envelope, already addressed and pre-stamped. Now all she has to do is perform a minor miracle and get it to the post office before it closes.

Mad is dressed in shorts and running shoes. Her long legs have filled out and no longer look skeletal. In fact, she positively oozes health and vitality.

"Do you think you'll make it?" I yell after her rapidly retreating form.

Mad is already halfway down our path and yells back, "Is the Pope Catholic?"

I laugh. There is no doubt we are all giving 'fate' a very determined helping hand.

It's Saturday morning and I am about to descend on the old Waiheke bach. Tony, Mum and Mad are all down at Blackpool Beach setting up the barbeque. Just before I left, I saw Mum slip her hand into Tony's. Mad caught my eye, giving me a conspiratorial wink.

I have walked up the road and I'm approaching the house from the front entrance, ignoring the dead-end fork that leads to the bush section at the back. Already I can see the curtains are all drawn, just the same as they had appeared that Saturday at the beginning of December last year. Then I notice the ancient rusty letterbox is no longer on a precarious lean. The lawns are also carefully mown, leaving an even pattern of long straight lines. I gave a smug grin. *Yep, someone is definitely home.*

I am about to knock on the front door but instinct stops me. Instead I walk down past the garage with its massive water butt and hop up onto the rear deck.

Bailey is reclining on a Cape Cod style wooden chair and he doesn't move when he sees me. But I watch a familiar lopsided smile start to form around the corners of his mouth. Inevitably, his eyes are hidden behind a dark pair of sunnies and on his lap sits the finished copy of *Atonement*.

I haven't seen him in almost a year, but all I say is: "So it arrived then?"

"Uh-huh. An hour ago. Good old New Zealand Post eh!"

I quietly take in his gaunt cheekbones. He had always been tall and slender in build but now bones protrude awkwardly from gangly limbs. His dyed hair has grown out and looks a lifeless dull brown colour. His skin is pale and anaemic. He'd pass as an extra in a zombie movie.

I am shocked.

More than I had been the first time I'd seen his burns.

More than I had been when I realised Madeleine was anorexic.

"How's Madeleine?" he asks suddenly, as if following my

train of thought.

"In a hell of a lot better condition than you, I'd say. Haven't you found anyone's sandwiches you could swipe on Waiheke?"

He gives a subdued laugh, but all he says is, "Nah."

I'm suddenly not sure what to say. I add as an afterthought, "Mad was amazing in Godspell."

"I know."

I look at him in surprise. "So that *was* you I saw, right at the back?"

He nods his head and gives me a half smile.

I take a moment to digest this. Now there are so many more questions running through my head, but all I actually ask is: "So what did you think of the last chapter of *Atonement*?"

He goes quiet and then finally whispers, "You changed it."

"Yeah. Never really liked your ending. Used a bit of artistic licence here and there."

"You completely *rewrote it,* J.D.!"

"Yep, I guess I did. So — you still haven't told me what you think?"

He inclines his head thoughtfully. "Some of your dialogue was a bit cheesy."

I shrug. "What can I say? I'm an artist, not a writer."

"Actually, some parts were completely unrealistic."

"You think?"

"Uh-huh. Like when the Lord Protector showed up at that beach and called his son, Proton, a hero and said he was proud of him. How unreal is that?"

"Mmm... I would have to strongly disagree with you there. I

liked that particular scene and, as co-author, would adamantly refuse to remove any part of it."

Bailey makes a grunt sound that is a perfect imitation of his father. He is not making this easy. He continues, "Then there's that part where the Lord Protector gets romantically involved with the mother of the young girl Proton rescued."

"You didn't like that bit either?"

"Pure Mills and Boon."

"Personally, I rather enjoy the occasional romantic novel."

Bailey gives another grunt. After what feels like an interminable silence, he says, "So tell me honestly, J.D. How much of your version do you think is firmly grounded in reality?"

"Honestly?"

"Uh-huh."

"Mmm... Well, let me see... by my reckoning... ninety-nine percent."

I see Bailey's mouth twitch. He takes off his dark glasses and I am able to look into his familiar brown eyes. There is a definite glimmer of hope mixed in with the dark shadows.

He asks, "So what's with the one percent?"

I smile and say, "Well, you know that final scene where Proton and the Lord Protector are finally reconciled at the beach and then they turn around and the rescued girl's mother serves them piles of hot dogs with lashings of onions and tomato sauce?"

He frowns, "Uh-huh."

"It's just... I'm not *entirely* sure how many hotdogs Proton *actually* got to eat. The older sister of the girl Proton once rescued had got her appetite back. I confess, it's all a bit hazy and a question of timing."

He raises an amused eyebrow. "Do you think if Proton had left his rocket ship immediately instead of dithering, he may have scored a few more?"

I look at him gravely and announce, "Without a doubt."

Bailey throws back his head and roars with laughter.

When he has finished laughing, I blurt out, "I'll never be able to replace her."

He looks at me in surprise and says, "Who?"

"Holly. I know I remind you of her."

He raises an eyebrow again, tilts his head and gives me a carefully considered look. "Initially, yes — your eyes are a similar deep blue... and of course there is the same age difference. But early on you said something that was a very J.D. thing to say. I stopped comparing — after that I only saw you."

"What on earth did I say?"

He grins, "You told me your name was 'Taker Hike'."

Now it's my turn to crack up laughing. I remember that moment in the kitchen — it was right at the very start of our friendship. We have shared so much since then... I feel a wonderful warm mixture of pleasure and relief.

"Speaking of names, I guess I shall have to get used to calling you Adam now."

"Do you think of me as Adam?"

"Nope. I confess you are still Bailey inside my head."

"I'm kind of used to it now too. Besides, Bailey Summer as

an author's name has more of a ring to it than Adam Remmus, don't you think?"

"Totally."

He looks hesitant. Then he says, "Do you think the Lord Protector would find that... objectionable or... offensive?"

He's frowning again and I'm no longer sure if we are talking about a simple name change. I word my reply carefully.

"I believe he would find that perfectly acceptable if it added to his son's happiness."

The frown disappears.

"That's settled then." He holds out his long writer's fingers and says, with a slight tremor in his voice, "Ready to go to a barbeque at the beach with me, J.D.?"

I wonder if he realises we are off to feed both wolves.

I think he does.

I grab his hand in mine, squeeze it and reply simply, "Bailey Summer, I thought you would never ask."

About the Author

N.K. Ashworth lives on Waiheke Island in New Zealand's beautiful Hauraki Gulf. She shares her quirky tower house with an exuberant bearded collie called Jester, Gypsy the cat, and nine white doves named after laundry detergents. She is a painter and sculptor of fantasy themes, has a BA in Art History and is the author of the *Island Legacy Trilogy*.